PENGUIN BOOKS
THE DISTORTED MIRROR

Rasipuram Krishnaswamy Laxman was born and educated in Mysore. Soon after he graduated from the University of Mysore, he began cartooning for the *Free Press Journal*, a newspaper in Bombay. Six months later he joined the *Times of India* as staff cartoonist, and has been with the newspaper for over fifty years. He has written and published numerous short stories, essays and travel articles, some of which are collected here. He has also written three works of fiction, *The Hotel Riviera*, *The Messenger* and *Servants of India*, all published by Penguin Books. Penguin has also published several collections of Laxman's cartoons in the series *The Best of Laxman* and *Laugh with Laxman*. *The Tunnel of Time*, Laxman's autobiography, is available from Penguin as well.

R.K. Laxman was awarded the prestigious Padma Bhushan by the Government of India. The University of Marathwada conferred an honorary Doctor of Literature degree on him. He has won many awards for his cartoons, including Asia's top journalism award, the Ramon Magsaysay Award, in 1984.

R.K. Laxman lives in Mumbai.

THE DISTORTED MIRROR
Stories, Travelogues, Sketches

R.K. Laxman

PENGUIN BOOKS

An imprint of Penguin Random House

PENGUIN BOOKS

USA | Canada | UK | Ireland | Australia
New Zealand | India | South Africa | China | Singapore

Penguin Books is part of the Penguin Random House group of companies
whose addresses can be found at global.penguinrandomhouse.com

Published by Penguin Random House India Pvt. Ltd
4th Floor, Capital Tower 1, MG Road,
Gurugram 122 002, Haryana, India

Penguin
Random House
India

First published in Viking by Penguin Books India 2003
Published in Penguin Books 2004

10 9 8 7 6 5 4 3 2

ISBN 9780143031338

Typeset in Gatineau by S.R. Enterprises, New Delhi

Printed at Repro India Limited

www.penguin.co.in

MIX
Paper from
responsible sources
FSC® C047271

This is a legitimate digitally printed version of the book and therefore might not
have certain extra finishing on the cover.

Contents

Short Stories

AN ACCIDENT

KAILAS CHECKED the mileage and was satisfied with the distance he had put between Gunny Daga and himself. He'd been driving almost ceaselessly from the moment he had left him sprawled on the sofa three nights ago.

The road wound through a thickly wooded part of the country which, as he raced along the tall trees, gradually gave way to shrubs and fields. Now lone farmsteads stood haplessly in the parched vastness of unyielding land.

Kailas marvelled at the country and felt grateful that it offered him such a protective expanse and variety in which he could render himself inconspicuous.

He saw a petrol pump and stopped. There were lorries laden with goods standing around, billowing diesel smoke and making belligerent noises. While his car was being attended to, Kailas went across the street to a little shop and bought a newspaper. Though it was a day old, he scanned its columns anxiously.

Then, returning to his car, he sat down and repeated the performance—this time more carefully, dropping each page he finished into the back seat. He was relieved that there was no news about his escape.

When he got set to resume his journey, he was happy to see the road stretch invitingly before him. Deciding to take advantage of the bright day to get as far away as he could before sundown, he took off like a jet on a runway.

The car wheels spun, whistling on the melting-hot tar surface, the wind hit the glass shield with the force of a gale, and wailed like a thousand unseen ghosts. The horizon quivered and danced in the heat and mirages of puddles receded, disappeared and reappeared as Kailas madly sped towards them, spurred on by the feel of brute power under his grip. The ground on either side became more and more blurred as it hurtled past him with the gathering speed of the car.

Suddenly he heard sounds of a thunderous flapping all around. Before he could react, something blocked the view of the road in front. His reflexes went into action and he slammed down the brakes. The car swung crazily and skidded, its steel frame shuddering as though its bolts would fly off.

When it ground to a halt, Kailas sat stunned, gripping the steering so hard it could have cracked his bones. All his nerves had gathered up into a concentrated tight knot. He had no idea what devilish force had dealt the blow and where.

Kailas then realized that he was looking at a sheet of the newspaper he had bought, spread out neatly on the steering-wheel, as if he had propped it up there to read!

There was another sheet lying limply on the space above the dashboard, partly covering the windshield and one more next to him on the seat. He turned and noticed in the rear seat a chaos of newspaper pages.

The angry hooting of a passing truck jerked Kailas back to reality. His car was standing at an odd angle, blocking the way.

After moving it out, he sat and began to reflect in horrified fascination on his fate if he had dashed against the fat tamarind tree nearby! He visualized his car in a shambles and himself in it reduced to a bloody pulp. The gory image sent a cold shiver down his back. No one would have believed that his death was caused by half a dozen newspaper sheets flying about madly and that one of them wrapping itself round his face had sent him crashing against the tree at more than a hundred kilometres an hour!

After a while Kailas resumed the journey and made sure that every scrap of paper was thrown out of the car. But he never felt at ease again as he drove on: imaginary noises of rustling papers and odd sounds harassed him and hindered his progress.

The sun had gone down, setting the western sky aflame and Kailas had still not passed a town where he felt he could rest for the night. Late at night, at last he came by a place so tiny that its sole excuse for

existence seemed to be a noisy cinema house with bright-coloured bulbs and garish posters. Part of the town was still awake, for the show had not ended.

He parked the car in front of Nehru Lodge, went in and asked for a room.

'Of course, sir. I will give the one on the other side. You will not be disturbed by the racket created by the cinema house.'

Kailas was pleased with the friendly proprietor and the cheerful atmosphere of the place.

The room was small. An iron cot and chair filled it entirely. There was a window overlooking the darkness outside and the walls were unevenly plastered. A snuff manufacturer's calendar hung on the wall as if to add elegance to the room, with a picture of a female nude standing knee deep in a brook. But provocative parts of her body had been discreetly airbrushed to a superb vagueness, perhaps evoking a feeling of disappointment in the eager viewer. However, some previous occupant had tried his hand at restoring the picture with a ballpoint pen.

Kailas went down the passage to the common bathroom and poured buckets of cold water over his head, soaped and scrubbed himself till his skin tingled with freshness. Returning to his room, he changed, took out a bottle of whisky and sat down to relax.

For the first time in many months, Kailas felt a sense of security and peace. With the money he had, he could enjoy this tranquillity for a long time. Chances of Daga tracing him to Nehru Lodge seemed remote.

His eyes fell on the nude in the calendar and curiously his thoughts turned to Dorine, the typist who had worked for Daga.

She had disappeared without a trace just a few days before Kailas had deserted Daga.

'That bitch has no loyalty. It is not safe to have her around,' Daga had complained often. He had felt the same about Kannan who slaved for him in all sorts of ways. He was found dead on a railway track one day. Daga had not even pretended to be shocked when the news was brought to him.

Kailas, sitting in a poky room in an obscure hotel, thanked his stars that he got away before Daga began to feel that he was a security risk too.

The next morning a clattering noise outside the window woke him. His watch showed 6 a.m. He felt oppressed at the thought of the day that seemed to stretch like a desert without an object in view.

The noise outside went on rhythmically. Kailas edged upto the window and saw a timber yard: trucks were unloading the logs.

Under a small corrugated shed, a man was sitting at a 'table' which was actually the stump of a log. A smaller version of it served as his chair.

It struck Kailas that the set would look smart at the poolside of the fancy mansions that Daga built as a contractor. He had very rich customers who could afford his prices and paid him in black. Kailas himself was greatly influenced by such a sentiment and this had resulted in the accumulation of unmanageable quantities of cash in his flat.

Daga used to come into his room and toss bundles of notes on the table, calling it his 'share' of the 'deal'. Although it was tremendously exciting in the beginning, excessive cash soon became a source of constant anxiety for them. Kailas saw no intelligent way of disposing it, except on alcohol, women and gambling.

Soon this kind of life sucked him deeper into the business of the underworld. He realized that, unknown to himself, he had moved on quietly from being a building contractor's partner to a culpable crook. Kailas was appalled to think that he had indeed become a mean accomplice to several shady activities including murder.

Daga's consuming hunger for money and the mindless manner in which he blew it up with all the vulgarity of a Roman orgy began to sicken Kailas. He wanted to get away from it all but fear of attracting Daga's fatal suspicion kept him performing like a circus dog in his troupe. There was nothing like a friendly parting from Daga. He had a knack of getting rid of inconvenient people and he considered it a treacherous act if anyone even thought of leaving him.

Tension and suspense mounted each day till it became unbearable. Kailas had worked himself to such a state that if Daga happened to turn and look at him full in the face, even casually, he panicked and went cold all over.

One day, in a spirit of drunken bravado, lolling in bed with Dorine, he had declared his plans to quit and had invited her to elope with him. A few days later, she disappeared without trace. It was then Kailas realized that the time had come for him to leave.

After one of the Roman banquets one night, when Daga lay sprawled on a sofa in a drunken stupor, Kailas saw his chance, packed his bag and left.

That was four days ago and Daga had no way of knowing that Kailas was in Nehru Lodge with nearly the entire subcontinent between them.

The trucks had unloaded and left, one by one. Kailas washed, changed and went down for breakfast.

At the table opposite him, a man sat writing in a bulky weather-beaten leather diary. He looked up and gave a friendly smile: small-town traits, reflected Kailas.

'You are occupying the upstairs room overlooking the timber yard, aren't you? My name is Naidu,' the man said.

Kailas was taken aback. 'How did you guess I was in that room, Mr Naidu?' he asked, really surprised.

'Not Mister Naidu. Just Naidu. I saw you at the window, watching the unloading,' Naidu grinned.

He was big and dark with curly silvery hair and moustache.

'People from big towns don't observe much,' he remarked, sounding pleasantly critical.

'I am not from any big town,' Kailas bluffed hurriedly.

'Never mind. Any town other than this is big. You won't find one smaller than this in the whole country. Your name, sir?'

Kailas was prepared for the question. 'Hem Kumar. Call me Kumar, please.'

They sat and chatted for a long time. Kailas learnt that Naidu was a timber merchant and that the government had leased out to him a nearby forest from where he got the logs.

Three weeks went by. One day, at the breakfast table, Naidu said to him, 'I want someone to mind the work at the other end, at the Forest Lodge. Someone reliable and trustworthy, Kumar.'

Then the conversation proceeded on semi-business lines and, at the end of it, Kailas accepted the offer.

The Forest Lodge was tucked away inside a jungle, some 50 kilometres away, off the trunk road. An hour's drive on an undulating dirt-track inside the jungle brought Kailas and Naidu to the lodge.

'During the British days, this used to be a hunting lodge, they say,' Naidu said.

It was a picturesque log house on wooden stilts with red tiles and large glass windows. Kailas surveyed it closely.

A man appeared from somewhere and carried the luggage in. 'He will cook, wash, sweep, dust . . . This is the sitting room, that is the bedroom . . . bathroom . . .' Naidu went on talking. 'Milk, vegetables come from a village nearby. No problem . . .'

Kailas liked his work: he spent the whole day in the open in the shade of the trees. His job was to get the cut logs numbered with white paint, enter the number in a book and send them on to Naidu through a driver at the end of the day. He also had to guard against theft and illegal transactions.

By sundown, all the lorries would be gone, leaving him alone with the silent jungle. He would go in, have a bath, fix a drink and sit and read—by the light of a kerosene lamp—the papers and magazines that Naidu regularly sent. When there was no work, he would sometimes pay a visit to Nehru Lodge, meet his old friends and shop around to replenish his stock of soap, toothpaste and liquor.

Kailas found it hard to believe that this idyllic life of his was for real and not some tricky dream. The forest became his constant companion and enchanted, he would observe its varying moods from dawn to the brooding starlit hours of the night. Each season held a different thrill for him, but he liked the fury of the monsoon best when the roaring tropical storm lashed and held the jungle in its grip and shook it to the roots.

As time passed, the fear of Gunny Daga softly faded and settled at the back of his mind as a mere comical episode. Even some of Daga's crooked ways began to strike him as funny and at the thought of them Kailas used to chuckle sometimes. Daga and all that he stood for felt like someone else's experience.

One evening, when the last truck had left, groaning under the weight of the logs, Kailas saw a black car at the far end of the rugged track leading out of the forest. It was bobbing up and down, glorifying the sunset with the brilliance of the golden dust it kicked up.

Nobody had ever visited him at that hour: even at that distance, he sensed something ominous about the vehicle nosing its way towards him.

He dashed into the cottage quickly. In an instant, he had slipped back in time into the grip of tormenting fear. His heart pounded vigorously, as if it had a pair of hands. Sweating and gasping, he stood behind the door. He heard the car come to a stop, the engine die, the door bang.

Then the man shouted: 'Hey Kailas, come and say hello to your guest!'

The guttural voice conveyed that it belonged to a drunk man.

Kailas came out and went through a series of predetermined acts: he pretended to disbelieve his eyes at first. Surprise and joy followed on recognizing who the stranger was and then came the ecstatic cry: 'Daga! Oh Daga!'

With arms spread out in a melodramatic gesture of welcome, he moved towards him.

'Shut up and get back into the house,' Daga shouted, dodging Kailas's embrace.

Kailas at once sprinted back into the sitting room, dragged the chairs around, cleared the table of all the accumulated papers, lit the lamps and was still fussing about and cackling like an old aunt when Daga thundered: 'Enough, you idiot! Sit down!'

'No, not before I fix you a drink,' Kailas said coyly.

Daga finished the drink at one draught. 'You have done yourself very well for a traitor,' he said, looking around with cynical appreciation.

'How is the drink—OK?' Kailas asked, refilling his glass and ignoring the remark.

'How much money have you made? I want the truth. I am not making a social call, you know. I am here on business.'

'Money? No money in this business, Daga. Only peace of mind,' Kailas replied, smiling tranquilly.

By now it was totally dark outside. The lamp in the room was attracting a stream of insects of all colours, sizes and shapes. Kailas got up and closed the wire-mesh windows and doors, muttering all the while about the difficult life he was leading, as if it was a punishment.

He knew Daga was not listening. Daga was staring fixedly at Kailas. He looked like a double-barrelled gun with a pair of eyes, Kailas thought.

'Where have you tucked away your lovey-dovey Dorine? Under your cot?' he gestured coarsely and roared with laughter.

Kailas's hand shook as he poured the drinks.

'You cowardly bastard. Never mind about the bitch. Tell me what happened to all the money. Donated it to an orphanage?'

'I did not have any money . . .' Kailas began, hopelessly trying an explanation.

'Liar!' Daga shouted. He pounded the table so hard the oil lamp nearly toppled over and both of them shot out their hands to save their glasses.

Daga was steadily losing control over himself. He demanded one drink after another in rapid succession. He shouted obscenities and abuses at the top of his voice. 'You son of a bitch. You give me my share. Fifty thousand cash—now! You think I did not know that you disposed of that consignment . . .'

'Fifty thousand!' Kailas gasped. 'Where am I to go . . .?'

'Go and steal it, if your life is that precious. But get it. If you run again, I will kill you, no matter which gutter you hide in. Tomorrow this time. Fifty thousand.'

Kailas sat paralysed. Daga was a killer and the hunting lodge was ideally suited for his operation. He could kill and walk away without a soul knowing it.

'Give me some more time,' Kailas mumbled tò fill a menacing silence.

'No. You wish to live or die—that is up to you to decide. I have no time to waste, I have a business deal to finish tonight. The party is waiting. I have a hundred bloody kilometres to go.'

'Have one for the road,' Kailas pleaded, desperately trying to keep him back and finding a perverted sense of safety in the company of his own murderer-to-be.

Daga stood up unsteadily and asked: 'Where is it . . .?'

Kailas took a lamp and conducted him to the toilet.

Kailas busied himself, clearing away the glasses, pushing the chair out of the way, picking up the scattered magazines and papers.

The newspaper sheets lying on the floor reminded him sharply of the day when they proved nearly fatal, flying about like evil spirits inside his speeding car.

He quickly gathered half a dozen of them and rushed out. Luckily, the doors of Daga's car were unlocked.

'It is only a chance in a million,' he told himself as, with trembling hands, he neatly spread out the sheets of a newspaper all over the rear seat at various strategic points and angles.

Then, taking care to lower the windows a little, he returned to the sitting room at lightning speed.

Daga had not come out of the toilet and was still making loud noises, clearing his throat and nose.

Finally he came out, wiping his face with a kerchief and cursing. 'Bloody darkness,' he mumbled.

'Tomorrow you will be dead if you don't have the money on you. Remember that and don't try to run . . . I will get you wherever you go . . .' he said with chilling casualness and stepped out into the dark.

Kailas heard the car start and saw briefly the trees bleached in the car's ghostly headlights, as if woken up from an ancient slumber. Then they vanished as it swung round and pulled away.

Kailas staggered into a chair as the significance of Daga's visit slowly descended on his mind like a load. The lamps fluttered and went out one by one and he sat crushed, staring into the darkness.

He had no idea when he had fallen asleep. The next morning he woke up with a start when the milkman called through the window: 'Sir, sir!'

The room was bathed in daylight and his watch showed 8 a.m.

'Why are you so late? Have the lorries come?'

'There was an accident on the highway. So I was delayed . . . A lot of crowd and police . . .'

'Where?'

The milkman flung his hand out and indicated a vague distance.

'A car had smashed against a tree. Luckily, there was no one in it except the driver. He was dead.'

'Who was he?'

'Don't know. I could not see the face. The police had covered it with a newspaper.'

THE DAY THE VICEROY
CAME

THAT MORNING Gopal's mother took out from a wooden box a little brown coat with brass buttons and yellow piping and put it on him; this happened only on great occasions. The smell of camphor and teak wood lifted his spirits; he smelt like his father, he thought, and that gave him an immense sense of importance. He picked up his slate and proudly strode out of the house. At school he joined the other children bubbling with joy in their own Sunday best.

The Viceroy of India was passing through the small town. He was to alight at the railway station with his spouse and immediately get into an elaborately decorated open coach drawn by well-groomed horses and drive straight to the Residency. From there, less conspicuously, in a sedan car, he was planning to escape to the hills for the summer.

Circulars had gone to all schools months in

advance instructing the authorities that all children should be presentably dressed and arrayed on either side of His Excellency's route on his arrival to cheer and welcome him appropriately. The headmasters and teachers were in a state of nervousness for fear that something might go wrong on that day and their institution betray a lack of loyalty in any respect. Special drill classes had been ordered and intensive and fatiguing training had been given to the children to participate in the great event.

Gopal, of course, was quite unaware of the importance of his role and the duty he was to discharge towards the Crown even as he was being marched to the railway station along with the other children. He was happy with the little chunk of sweet distributed to celebrate the occasion and liked the festive mood that had infected everyone in the school; even the drill master wore a smile and went about, his muscles relaxed.

At the railway station the children were lined up on the footpath according to their size and shape, the better dressed ones in the front row.

Gopal was giddy with expectation and suspense. The drill master strutted up and down the line as if he was reviewing an army parade. He talked to people with the air of a liaison officer; even the headmaster consulted him and took his advice on many points connected with the arrangements. Every few minutes he looked at his huge wristwatch and announced the exact position of the approaching Viceregal party. But an hour passed without anything happening. The children began to get restless and clamoured for His Excellency's arrival. The drill master admonished the noisy ones and sauntered away to find out the cause for the delay.

But as time wore on the sun grew irksome. The whole assembly began to droop. The teachers, one by one, sought the cool shade of the avenue trees. The children squatted on the ground in groups and wilted in the heat.

As Gopal viewed his companions languidly and was about to resign himself to boredom he felt a ticklish sensation in his left leg. He was startled to see a big black ant crawling up. He jumped about as if he had stepped on a live coal and managed to shake it off. It gyrated blindly and came towards him again.

Gopal pushed it away with a small twig. But it returned brandishing its whiskers with vicious intent. He became annoyed with its obstinacy and flicked it away a little more savagely. The ant landed far away and rolled in the dust.

Gopal was pleased; he waited for its next move with fascination. It recovered immediately and seemed to go mad with frustration. It picked up the scent and moved towards him like an enemy tank in a battlefield.

So expressive was its fury that Gopal had a momentary misgiving about his own strength to cope with it. He hurriedly gathered a handful of sand and

emptied it on the charging ant.

It came out of the temporary burial vastly puzzled by Gopal's new tactics.

Gopal felt a mixture of triumph and compassion. He gently picked up the bewildered ant on the twig. It clung to it and remained still as if admitting defeat.

Then it began to pick its way carefully along the slender stick. It came very close to his fingers; it would have climbed on to him, actually, if he had not let go his fingers at that moment and held the stick by the other end. The ant suddenly faced an abyss. Then it turned round and started walking back towards Gopal's fingers. But Gopal repeated the trick, shifting his fingers in time to the other end of the stick. He liked this game and it went on unvaryingly for a long time.

Then suddenly he heard a blare of trumpets and the band striking up '*God Save The King*'. There was a lot of rush and bustle around him. He turned his attention from the ant to his friends; they were already at the edge of the footpath standing in a line.

He was about to drop the twig, ant and all and rejoin his friends when he discovered to his horror that the ant which ought to have been somewhere near his finger was nowhere to be seen! He shivered with fright at the thought that it could have climbed over his fingers and got lost in his sleeves. He frantically looked for it all over his coat and on the ground.

It had completely vanished.

With an uneasy feeling he joined the group. But

His Excellency, the Viceroy of India had already gone.

The gathering dispersed rapidly. 'I saw him so close,' announced one of his friends.

'I liked the horses,' said another.

'He is no doubt a man with a great personality,' Gopal heard the drill master remark.

At home his mother asked as she removed his coat to fold it and put it back into the wooden box, 'Did you have a nice time?'

'Yes.'

'Did you have a good look at the Viceroy?'

'No.'

'Why?'

'I was busy.'

A TOUCH OF FEVER

SHANTHA'S MOTHER felt her forehead and declared, 'You have fever. Go and lie down quietly somewhere, and stop following me around.'

Lie down quietly, where? Shantha wondered. There was not an inch of space in the house which was not occupied by guests who had been pouring in for the wedding, crowding the house from the garage, fuel room and kitchen in the rear to the main hall and veranda in the front, according to their status. The kitchen was buzzing with cooks who stamped about with heavy feet, carrying amazingly big vessels with boiling liquids in them. They glistened with sweat and themselves looked boiled in the heat of the kitchen. Shantha's mother was part of a busy force of women slicing an enormous quantity of vegetables or shaping fancy eatables. Shantha realized wearily the futility of trying to draw her mother's attention.

The main hall had totally lost its familiar look. There was even some sort of a little mud construction in the middle surrounded by an elaborate floral design in rice paste. The rest of the space was occupied by men drinking coffee, chewing paan and chattering away. Shantha moved to the front veranda. Here, old men sat completely relaxed, reading the newspaper or just fanning themselves. Shantha avoided these people. These people had an annoying tendency to call little children of her size at sight and ask them to fetch a glass of water or their spectacles or to find out the whereabouts of somebody. She stood concealed from their view behind a pillar and watched the children of all ages and sizes jumping, running and screaming madly out of joy under the cool shade of the huge colourful wedding pandal. Her head throbbed, her eyes burned, her limbs seemed heavy as lead. Somehow, looking at all the energy of the children overpowered her with fatigue. Her immediate need was to quietly curl up somewhere and sleep. She found a place in the hall between a huge basket of flowers covered with a wet cloth and a heap of coconuts in brown paper bags. Hardly did she lie down when a voice called out, 'Hey, Shantha, couldn't you find a better place to lie down? You are in the way. Go and find another place.' The half a dozen places she tried after that were no better; she was in the way, she was told, and was asked to find another place. It was maddening. There seemed to be no alternative left to her but to withdraw to the centre of the busy hall and start crying as hard as she could. It was the only way to pass on to her mother the job of finding a place for her to sleep, she decided. But just then it occurred to her that she could go upstairs and find a quiet and comfortable place. The proposition, besides, contained an element of thrill of doing something she was forbidden to do; she was not allowed to climb the narrow steep steps unescorted by an elder.

Actually, the top floor contained no rooms. There was just a small landing with a door leading to an open terrace. The landing was generally used as a sort of a family 'bedroom'; all the beddings of the members of the family were rolled and piled up one on top of another out of sight here during the day and brought down and spread out for sleeping at night. Shantha noticed that the landing was choked with rolls and rolls of bedding. 'Wedding guests,' she murmured with a frown. But she was relieved to find the place free of people. Here, at last, she could rest her aching limbs and throbbing head and, above all, go to sleep. She wanted to make doubly sure that her hard-won seclusion would not be lost if someone happened to come upstairs. So she climbed over the rolls of bedding like a little mountaineer, risking tumbling down at every step. The spirit of adventure freshened her up a little. Panting with excitement, she levered herself on to the topmost roll of bedding. Shantha felt triumphant that none of her friends had scaled anything so high. She lay down and adjusted herself snugly in the gentle depression between the wall and the mattress. Now she was totally hidden from any chance visitor upstairs. She felt completely relaxed. She listened to the sounds from below: someone was arguing violently, some elderly female was describing the most economical way to see certain holy places which she had just been to, a music lover was demonstrating how to sing a particular song as well as how not to sing it, many children were howling in various parts of the house. All these sounds gradually merged and lulled Shantha to sleep.

When Shantha awoke the sun had set. The room was dissolving into the soft half-tone of dusk. For a moment Shantha could not make out where she was. She would have continued to sleep if she had not been roused by voices very close to her, just on the other side of the hump of the mattress concealing her from view. She could make out a male voice and a female voice. Both were engaged in conversing in suppressed agitation: 'I called you here; I have something to tell you and I can't do that down there without a hundred lounging louts overhearing me.'

'Be brief and tell me what it is.'

'I have nothing to tell. I have something to show. Look!'

'Oh! Where did you get it?'

'I found it. In the bathroom as I was washing my hands after lunch in the afternoon. It was on the rack where the soap . . .'

'Whose is it?'

'What a question! How would I know? Must belong to some queen rich enough to throw it away in the bathroom every time she takes a bath.'

'What are you going to do with it?'

'Nice question to ask me! That is just what I want to know. Why did you think I called you here?'

'Return it, I suppose.'

'Return it to whom? Do you expect me to render free detective service to this house? As if the expense we have incurred in coming for this grand wedding was not sufficient.'

'And at the end of it how will you be sure it is the right owner you will be returning it to?'

'Exactly. If I had not discovered it, some smart guest surely would have quietly appropriated it and would have more than recovered the expenditure of coming to this grand wedding . . .'

'What about the cost of buying some suitable gift for the bride and the groom? It will not at all look nice if we do not place something on the tray and offer it to the couple. After all, whatever it is, we have to save face on occasions like this . . .'

Shantha, by now, had become quite curious to have a glimpse of the people who were talking in such mysterious hushed voices. But instinctively she felt the need for caution. She could judge their identity from their voices. They were relatives of some sort on her father's side. But they were objects of much discussion and quarrels as long as Shantha could remember.

'Where are you going to keep it—in your pocket?'

'Don't be silly. Of course, in my trunk.'

'But there are about a thousand people around your trunk in that hall at the moment. How are you going to put it there? Don't blunder and make a fool of yourself. Already people are jealous of us, you must remember.'

'If you are so wise why don't you take charge of it?'

'What, me? I certainly won't. Please leave me out of it.'

'If you feel so afraid, go and leave it in the bathroom where you found it . . .'

'Then suggest some way out. We can't spend the whole evening talking here. They may soon miss us downstairs.'

'Anyway, my box is out of the question. A hundred curious eyes peep into my box whenever I open it as if they expect to find all the property of their grandfathers in it.'

'I am asking you to suggest a place to keep it—not the impossibilities.'

'Keep it in your pocket till nightfall. When everyone goes to bed you can open your box and pop it in.'

'Suppose it falls out or somebody sees it? I can't take that risk . . . Ah, I have an idea! My bedding must be somewhere here. There it is. I will keep this inside one of these pillowcases now and roll it up in the bed and leave it here. At night anyhow I have to take the bedding down. When everyone goes to sleep, I can transfer it to my box easily . . .'

For the next few minutes Shantha heard a rustle of bed sheets and thumping of pillows. Suddenly she saw a huge roll of bedding settle with a thud a few inches from her. A dark thick hand appeared and patted it twice for safety and withdrew. Then she heard footsteps going down the stairs. The place became quiet again except for the noise of the wedding house which was gathering tempo for the event in the morning.

Shantha extricated herself from the corner into which she was wedged and sat up. She surveyed the awesome roll of bedding with fascination. The rug it was wrapped in was chocolate in colour with yellow diamonds running along the border. She discovered other geometrical shapes and colours as she came closer and closer to examine it.

Everyone was fussing around Shantha. She had not been seen the whole day. All the guests had finished their dinner and had gathered in the central hall. Shantha was lying luxuriously on her grandmother's lap. Her grandmother was coaxing her to drink milk from a spoon. Shantha was resisting. 'You are a good

girl. Come and drink it up. You have not had a thing to eat since the morning. Where will you have the strength to participate in the wedding tomorrow? You must get well and put on the new blue skirt for the wedding. Come on, drink it up. You are a brave girl . . . I will tell everyone you are a good girl.' The grandmother put the tumbler and spoon down and clapped her hands and drew everybody's attention. All the men and women turned to her with mild expectation.

'Shantha is a good girl. Look at this gold chain! It is made of ten *tolas* of solid gold. You will not get this sort of thing nowadays. It was given to my mother by her uncle when I was born. I left it in the bathroom this morning and totally forgot about it. Little Shantha told me she found it there and brought it back to me. Ten tolas! God is truly great . . .' Shantha reached for the glass of milk while her grandmother was still making the speech and concentrated all her attention on drinking the milk.

THE LETTER

BHASKER SAT cross-legged on the ancient chair in front of his roll-top desk and slid back the top after a brief tussle with its rusty mechanism. The inside revealed a fantastic arrangement of pigeon-holes, drawers and tiny doors. With a little creative indulgence he could have even seen in it mysterious passages, dark corridors, narrow alleys, balconies and house-tops, as he used to do some sixty years ago perched on his grandfather's knee as the old man busied himself with the papers in a pigeon-hole of the same old desk.

Bhasker took out a fat file from one of the drawers. It opened like the bellows of a camera, each fold like a compartment for papers. He held it upside down and emptied the contents on the green felt top of the table. The idea was to destroy the unwanted papers and arrange and classify the rest. This was not the first time that an attempt was being made towards this end. He'd tried it several times over the years, but each time had been lost in the contents of various papers and letters and after several hours had got up after putting all the papers back into the file again.

Bhasker was a great one for preserving letters, which according to his definition meant every bit of paper that passed through his hands. There was a time when he would not throw away even handbills announcing drama shows. Weeks after a journey he would still feel a deep attachment to a railway ticket. Though this passion gradually tapered off as he grew old he was still in possession of a formidable collection of old letters, marriage invitation cards, doctors' prescriptions, recipes for special kinds of pickles which cured stomach ailments and a heap of papers of an indefinite nature.

When his obsession was at its peak, even the loss of a routine club circular had caused much tension at home—hot exchanges among members of the family—and ended quite often with the little ones being spanked for converting the circular into a paper boat. Bhasker firmly believed that all letters should be preserved for a week before their usefulness was scrutinized, and then destroyed or filed. But in practice only a very few were removed and the bulk survived for another week, another, and yet another, until he developed a sentimental attachment to them; then they acquired a status high enough to enter the protective folds of the big file and remained there, yellowing with age. He felt like a vandal damaging an antique if he were to destroy even a single bit of paper from the precious collection.

But that morning Bhasker approached the file with a grim determination without letting the excuse of their age or his memories protect them.

The first paper he came across was a telegram dated 16 March 1927, from Thalivanam, a gritty hot village whose architecture and temperature, Bhasker remembered, were like those of a mud oven. The message in the telegram said: 'GOD'S GRACE. SHARADA GAVE BIRTH TO MALE CHILD. MOTHER AND CHILD WELL. LETTER FOLLOWS.'

It was the announcement of the birth of his first son, who was now in Delhi conducting research into a new strain of rice which would solve the nation's food problem in twenty years. He had even been invited to Geneva to read papers before some important world body.

The thought of this son always warmed Bhasker's heart as he was a contrast to the second son who, after marrying a rich girl, never did a stroke of work and made a fool of himself, letting her openly lead him by the nose. But he was a good sportsman in his day. The glass case in the hall was full of silver trophies of all sizes and shapes won by him. The thought of the trophies made Bhasker feel a little charitable—after all, the young fellow was not a bad sort; it was his mother who spoilt him.

He kept the telegram aside and picked up a thick gilt-edged emblem-embossed card. It was an invitation addressed to his father to a civic reception arranged in honour of '. . . His Excellency Sir Maurice Baring, KCIE, Governor of . . .'

Next was a letter from Bhasker's mother written to him when he was studying in Madras. He ran his eyes over the letter: ' . . . and do not fail to take oil bath every week and drink plenty of milk before going to bed . . . I read somewhere that milk has the medicinal property of a hundred apples . . .' It went on thus for nearly two pages.

Then there were quite a few bills of 1920 vintage from the Southern Silk Emporium and the National Provision Stores, both of which had disappeared long ago under a road-broadening scheme launched by the local municipality. For a second the image of his daughter on the morning of her wedding day came to his mind: shy, bedecked in flowers, looking absurdly small, she was almost lost in the billowing brocade sari supplied by the Southern Silk Emporium. She herself had a daughter now of marriageable age and three brilliant sons poised to take off to various corners of the USA and Germany for higher technical training.

As he was thinking of his daughter his eyes fell on a piece of paper on which was written: 'Sandalwood powder, Claws of a cat, Camphor . . .' It was a recipe for making incense sticks. He had copied it from a book as a boy with the hope of becoming financially independent of his father by manufacturing and selling his own brand of incense sticks. The project collapsed for want of raw materials; except camphor he could get no other ingredient.

He reached for a pink letter on the heap and unfolded it. He realized with a start that it was a letter written by him in a juvenile hand nearly half a century ago. He remembered writing it sitting close to a railway track in a wide field under a burning sun.

That was the morning the SSLC exam results were announced. For the second year running Bhasker did not find his number in the paper. His father had not only hired three high-powered private tutors to reinforce his son's own efforts to understand biology, Sanskrit and algebra, but had promised to thrash him within an inch of his life if he failed to get a first class. Now he had not even got a class! He had failed totally!

And his father was a man of his word. Bhasker saw his father advancing towards him, eyes burning with anger, nostrils dilated, bellowing, and finally pouncing on Bhasker! The picture sent him fleeing to the rail track in terror.

The 11.15 Thindivanam passenger passed that way if it was punctual. Bhasker finished writing the note and surveyed the field. There was nothing in sight, except a lame donkey in search of grass. Far away the conical shapes of the important buildings of the town quivered in the simmering heat of the sun.

He folded the letter carefully and put it in his pocket. He thought of the news item that would appear in the local paper: ' . . .a note found on the mutilated body indicated that the deceased took his own life . . .'

He thought of his mother; she was the only one who would really suffer; the whole house would be plunged in gloom. A sudden surge of self-pity engulfed him for a moment. He could not imagine his father feeling sorry for Bhasker; on the other hand he would perhaps keep his appointment at the bridge table at the club. He would not miss that, not even when his son perished under the wheels of the Thindivanam passenger.

If his father had been a little more sensible, Bhasker would have been home by now, had his lunch, and be lounging in the easychair, poring over the *Sports Weekly*, instead of waiting for the train to solve his educational problem. He wondered what they would do with his personal things. He felt relieved that he did not take his bicycle along to see the results that morning; he would have had to abandon it here on the field. Cycle thieves were doing a roaring business everywhere; but he had taken the precaution of scratching his initials in seven secret places all over his bicycle.

A distant whistle pierced his thoughts. He was startled. His whole body throbbed like one big agitated heart. Beads of perspiration gathered over his brows and flowed down. The train had left the city station and would arrive here any moment.

The sun was high in the sky, pouring down heat and light on the landscape with elemental fury, melting all colour and form to a mass of white heat. It became unbearable for Bhasker. He gazed steadily at the spot where the train would appear. His head ached; his eyes smarted with the glare. He turned away for a brief second of relief and the lame donkey caught his attention.

The chugging of the approaching train came faintly from a distance. Bhasker saw it and involuntarily moved away a little. It grew menacingly bigger every second. Suddenly he was seized with panic and confusion; he did not know at what point one introduced one's head to the wheels of the monstrously huge train. He was overwhelmed by its speed and noise as it thundered past him. Bhasker watched the carriages loyally clank past. And soon he saw the last carriage hurrying away with a gentle sway and disappearing around the bend.

Sitting at the roll-top desk that morning, Bhasker glanced through the suicide note: ' . . . My dear father and mother . . . Cruel fate . . . I have no alternative . . . miserable existence . . . time will heal . . . worthless son . . . relief to all . . .'

Bhasker chuckled to himself as he folded the letter and put it back in the file. He gathered all the other letters in one sweep, stuffed them back into it and rolled down the top of the desk.

THE GOLD FRAME

THE MODERN FRAME WORKS was actually an extra-large wooden packing case mounted on wobbly legs tucked in a gap between a drug store and a radio repair shop. Its owner, Datta, with his concave figure, silver-rimmed glasses and a complexion of seasoned timber, fitted into his shop with the harmony of a fixture.

He was a silent, hard-working man. He gave only laconic answers to the questions his customers asked and strongly discouraged casual friends who tried to intrude on his zone of silence with their idle gossip. He was always seen sitting hunched up, surrounded by a confusion of cardboard pieces, bits of wood, glass sheets, boxes of nails, glue bottles, paint tins and other odds and ends that went into putting a picture in a frame. In this medley a glass-cutter or a pencil stub was often lost and that was when he would uncoil from his posture and grope impatiently for it. Many times he had to stand up and shake his dhoti vigorously to dislodge the lost object. This operation rocked the whole shop, setting the pictures on the walls gently swinging.

There was not an inch of space that was not covered by a picture; gods, saints, hockey players, children, cheap prints of the Mona Lisa, national leaders, wedding couples, Urdu calligraphy, the snow-clad Fujiyama and many others coexisted with a cheerful incongruity like some fabulous world awaiting order and arrangement.

A customer standing outside the shop on the pavement, obstructing the stream of jostling pedestrians, announced, 'I want this picture framed.' Datta, with his habitual indifference, ignored him and continued driving screws into the sides of a frame. 'I want a really good job done, no matter how much it costs.' The customer volunteered the information, unwrapping a faded newspaper and exposed a sepia-brown photograph of an old man. It was sharp and highly glazed in spite of its antiquity.

'What sort of a frame would you like?' Datta asked, still bent over his work.

'The best, of course. Do you expect I would stint where this great soul is concerned?'

Datta glanced sideways and caught a glimpse of the photograph: just another elderly person of those days, he told himself: a standard portrait of a grandfather, a philanthropist, a social worker, with the inevitable whiskers and top-heavy cascading turban—it could be any one of these. At least half a dozen people came to him every month bearing similar portraits, wanting to demonstrate their homage to the person in the picture in the shape of a glittering frame.

The customer was describing the greatness of the old man: extravagant qualities of nobility, compassion, and charity were being generously attributed to him in a voice that came close to the chanting of a holy scripture ' . . . If this world had just a few more like him, believe me, it would certainly have been a different place. Of course, there are demons who may not agree with me. They are out to disgrace his name and destroy his memory. But he is God in my home!'

'What sort of a frame do you want?' Datta interrupted. 'Plain, wooden, lacquer, gold, plastic or just enamel painted?' He waved a casual hand towards the pictures on the wall. The customer silently surveyed the various frames. After some time Datta heard him mumble, 'I want the best . . .'

'I don't have any second-rate stuff in my shop,' Datta said.

'How much will that gold frame cost?' enquired the customer.

He was shown a number of samples: plain, decorative, floral, geometrical, thin, hefty and so forth. The customer was baffled by the variety. He examined the selection before him for a long time and seemed afraid of enshrining his saviour for ever in some ugly cheap frame.

Datta came to his rescue and recommended one with a profusion of gold leaves and winding creepers and, in order to clear any lingering doubt he might still harbour in regard to its quality, added: 'It is German! Imported!'

The customer at once seemed impressed and satisfied. Datta next asked, 'You want a plain mount or a cut mount?' and watched the puzzled look return. Again he helped the man out by showing his various mounts and suggested that a cut mount looked more elegant.

'All right, let me have a cut mount then. Is that a cut mount?' he asked, pointing to a framed picture on the wall of a soulful-looking lady in an oval cut mount. 'I like that shape. Will it cost much?'

'No. Frame, mount, glass—all will cost seventeen rupees.'

The customer had expected it would be more. He pretended to be shocked all the same and tried to bargain. Datta withdrew to his corner without replying and began to cut a piece of plywood. The customer hung about uncertainly for some time and finally asked, 'When will you have it ready?' and barely heard the reply over the vibrating noise of the saw on the plywood, 'Two weeks from today.'

Datta had learnt by experience that his customers never came on the day of delivery. They came days in advance and went away disappointed or came months later, and some never turned up at all and their pictures lay unclaimed in a box, gathering dust and feeding cockroaches and silver fish. Therefore, he only made frames for those who visited him at least twice before he actually executed their orders.

Ten days later the tall, rustic-looking man appeared and enquired, 'Has the picture been framed? I was passing by and thought I could collect it if it was ready.'

Datta cast a sideways look at him and continued with his work. 'I know I have come four days early,' the customer grinned nervously. 'Will it be ready by Tuesday?'

Datta merely nodded without shifting attention from a tiny nail which he, with precise rhythmic strokes, was driving into a frame. He, however, sensed the man's obsessive attachment to the photograph. He told himself there would be trouble if he did not deliver the order on the promised date.

Next morning he made that his first job, keeping aside all the others.

The photograph was lying on a shelf among many others. He took it and carefully kept it on a wooden plank on the floor. Then he looked for the pencil stub for marking the measurements. As usual it was missing. He swept his hand all round him impatiently, scattering fragments of glass and wood.

False shapes that he mistook for the pencil harassed him no end and stoked his anger. Frustrated in all his attempts to find it, he finally stood up to shake the folds of his dhoti—an ultimate move which generally yielded results. But he shook the folds so violently that he upset a tin containing white enamel paint and it fell right on the sacred photograph of the old man, emptying its thick, slimy contents on it.

Datta stood transfixed and stared at the disaster at his feet as if he had suddenly lost all faculty of movement. He could not bring himself even to avert his eyes from the horror which he seemed to be cruelly forced to view. Then his spectacles clouded with perspiration and helpfully screened his vision.

When at last he fully recovered his senses he set about rescuing the picture in such desperate hurry that he made a worse mess of it. He rubbed the picture so hard with a cloth that he peeled off thin strips of filmy coating from its surface. Before he realized what he had done half the old man's face and nearly all of his turban were gone. Datta helplessly looked at the venerable elder transformed into thick black specks sticking to the enamel smeared on the rag in his hand.

He sat, clutching his head with both hands; every vein in his head throbbed, and his head felt like it would burst if he did not hold it down with his hands. What answer was he going to offer to the customer who had a fanatic devotion to the photograph he had just mutilated beyond recovery? His imagination ran wild, conjuring nightmarish consequences to his own dear self and to the fragile inflammable shop.

He racked his brain for a long while till sheer exhaustion calmed his agitated nerves and made him accept the situation with hopeless resignation. Meanwhile the plethora of gods, saints and sages gazed down at him from the walls with transcendental smiles and seemed to offer themselves to him to pray to. With a fervent appeal in his heart he stared at them.

In his muddled state of mind he did not realize for quite a while that a particular photograph of a person on the wall had held his attention more than it was qualified to do. It was an ordinary portrait of a middle-aged man in a dark suit and striped tie, resting his right arm jauntily on a studio prop made to look like a fluted Roman pillar. Datta was amazed to see that he had a faint likeness to the late lamented old man. The more he gazed at the face the more convincing it appeared to him. But he dismissed the odd resemblance he saw as one of those tricks of a thoroughly fagged-out mind. All the same, at the back of his mind an idea began to take shape: he saw the possibility of finding an acceptable substitute!

He brought down the old wooden box in which he had kept all the photographs unclaimed over the years. As he rummaged in it, panicky cockroaches and spiders scurried helter-skelter all over the floor. Unmindful of

them, Datta anxiously searched for the brownish
photographs of the old man's vintage. Soon there was
a pile before him: he was surprised he could pick up
so many which qualified to take the old man's place.
But he had to reject a lot of them. In most of the
portraits the subjects sported a very conspicuous flower
vase next to them, or over-dressed grandchildren sat
on their laps and therefore had to be rejected. Luckily,
there was one with which Datta felt he could take a
fair risk; the print had yellowed a bit noticeably but he
calculated that the total effect when put in a dazzling
gold frame would render it safe.

After a couple of hours' concentrated work he sat
back and proudly surveyed the old man's double,
looking resplendent in his gold frame. He was so
pleased with his achievement that he forgot he was
perhaps taking one of the greatest risks any frame
maker ever took! He even became bold enough to
challenge the customer if his faking was discovered.
'Look, my dear man,' he would say, 'I don't know who
has been fooling you! That's the picture you brought
here for framing. Take it or throw it away!'

The days that followed were filled with suspense
and anxiety. Datta feared that the customer would
surprise him at an unguarded moment making him
bungle the entire, carefully-thought-out plot. But the
man turned up promptly a couple of days later. At
that moment Datta was bent over a piece of work and

slightly stiffened as he heard the voice, shrill with expectation, ask, 'Is it ready?'

Datta's heart began to race and to compose himself he let a whole minute pass without answering. Then he put aside the scissors in his hand with slow deliberation and reached out to take the neatly wrapped package in a corner.

'Ah, it is ready!' the customer exclaimed with childish delight, at the same time mumbling flattering tributes to Datta for his promptness and so on. He spread his arms widely with dramatic exuberance to receive the photograph as if it was actually a long-lost person he was greeting.

But Datta took his time removing the wrapper from the frame. The customer waited impatiently, filling in the time showering more praises on his worshipful master who was to adorn the wall of his home.

Datta finally revealed the glittering frame and held it towards him. The customer seemed visibly struck by its grandeur and fell silent like one who had entered the inner sanctum of a temple.

Datta held his breath and watched the man's expression. With every second that passed he was losing his nerve and thought that in another moment he would betray the big hoax he had played.

Suddenly, he saw the customer straighten, the reverential look and benevolent expression vanished from his face.

'What have you done?' he demanded, indignantly. For Datta the moment seemed familiar for he had already gone through it a thousand times night and day since he splashed the white paint on the original photograph. He had rehearsed his piece several times precisely for this occasion. But before he could open his mouth the customer shouted with tremendous authority in his bearing, 'Now, don't deny it! I clearly remember asking for a cut mount with an oval shape. This is square, look!'

Travelogues

IDLE HOURS IN THE USA

I ENTERED one of those mammoth department stores to buy a toothbrush. My eyes caught a giant flower vase kept in the centre for decoration with colourful cascading flowers, leaves and creepers. I moved automatically towards it to smell the flowers and touch the leaves to find out if they were real.

This had indeed become a pastime with me wherever I went about in the United States. I would stop in the street and even scratch the avenue trees to test their genuineness. This habit started one day when I was leaning against a tree waiting for a friend outside an internationally well-known bank. It was a nice clear day; the sun was warm, the sky was blue and the tree was young and green. I casually reached for a little tender leaf which was fluttering in the cool breeze. What I touched was a lifeless piece of plastic! To my horror I discovered the whole tree was phony; it was made of wood and plastic.

I had, of course, on other occasions tried to take apples or grapes from ornate silver bowls at dining tables and felt like a fool at the feel of the hard chilly surface of the succulent plastic fruit. But I did not imagine that the synthetic garden of this country had grown so big as to have plastic trees.

And now, in this department store the flower vase held, as I had expected, dahlias, azaleas, roses and tulips, all fashioned out of plastic. But here something else startled me: hidden among these flowers I saw a camera-like contraption staring at me through its powerful lens and making a sickly whirring noise. I quickly withdrew, bewildered.

Thousands of shoppers were rushing about hugging their parcels and shopping bags, going up and down the escalators and running all over the place indulging in another bout of frenzied buying of clothes, kitchen gadgets, lawnmowers, ties, Mother's Day cards and rubber canoes. The staggering dimension of their buying capacity and the range of their needs would have continued to engage my thoughts had I not noticed another camera-like device staring at me from the ceiling from behind the electric lights. This one was majestically revolving, taking a sweep of the crowds below.

I forgot the toothbrush which I had come to buy and enthusiastically set about looking for hidden cameras. I found several during my hunt, peeping out of various improbable places. Some revolved, some oscillated, and some kept a steady gaze at customers through holes in the wall and from behind curtains. I was still ignorant about the purpose and nature of these objects. The more I spotted the more mysterious they grew. But my curiosity ended abruptly as I came across a huge sign on the wall which said: 'For the purpose of security the management has installed closed-circuit TV cameras at various places in this store . . .' This announcement was obviously meant for shoplifters who, I was told, walked away with millions of dollars worth of goods every year from supermarkets and department stores all over the USA. If anyone was tempted by the atmosphere of freedom that the system of self-service created and pocketed even a pair of nylon stockings, he would be nabbed at the exit. And yet, I understood that despite Big Brother watching them unblinkingly, adventure-loving teenagers, kleptomaniacs and common thieves merrily filch all kinds of things— from tie-pins to tractors.

'These are the afflictions and worries of affluence,' a hippie despondently explained to me later when I happened to tell him about my visit to the department store. The man's material needs did not seem to extend even to combs, blades and bath soaps.

I was sitting in a quiet corner in a park, watching children play in a pond with their radio-controlled toy boats when this hippie came and sat next to me. This was unusual because I thought hippies seldom left their pack. There were quite a few of his ilk gambolling on the grass, looking like soiled gods and angels in a second-class paradise. Some of them wore no shoes or sandals. Dark sunglasses and miles of beads round their necks seemed to be a ritualistic must in their way of life. A grisly beard was the only index to sex; otherwise males and females looked alike in their appearance and behaviour.

I scrutinized the hippie sitting next to me without any fear that I would be misunderstood for staring at him with such open curiosity. I believed all hippies loved to be stared at, frowned upon and generally talked about; they would languish without public attention to sustain them. He was wearing a black turtleneck pullover, strings of coloured glass beads, bells and buttons, with slogans crying out for a better world. His trousers were sliced off, as if with a pair of blunt scissors, crudely just below the knee. His hair and beard looked like a raw stock of wool for making dirty-brown woollen carpets.

He smiled at me with benign amusement as I looked for more items of interest on his person. I returned the smile, out of surprise at the unexpected human quality in the depth of all that fur. He appeared a trifle elderly for a hippie. He made enquiries about me and slowly began to talk.

I learnt a great deal about his philosophy and ambitions. He told me that his sole desire was to be a poor man. He hated affluence and comfort. In his personal life he had done away with furniture and carpets in his apartment. Books, clothes, paintings and crockery were kept in grand disorder all over the floor. His children went to a very ordinary overcrowded school in the neighbourhood. His wife bought clothes

only when needed, four times a year or so, and at bargain sales. His family ate its breakfast or dinner off the cooking range or refrigerator, standing, without bothering to sit at a table.

'You see how free I am. A poor man is free and has no obligations and responsibilities . . .'

He further declared that if an electric iron or a blender or any electric appliance went out of order he never threw it away; he repaired it himself and used it again. Finally he said, 'I have not changed even my car though it is nearly five years old . . .' and proudly thumped his chest; the bells jingled and the glass beads tinkled. I sat dumbfounded and amazed at the effort one has to put in that country to remain poor!

When I came across a friend and his son in New York I realized how difficult it was to pursue poverty in that land of opportunities. If that hippie I met in the park did not watch out, prosperity would sweep him off and he would end up as the vice-president of some industry or other and live forever suffering from affluence.

I had known this friend in India some fifteen years ago when he was here as the sales manager of an American company. He beamed with delight and warmth at our encounter and drove me in his luxurious European car to his suburban home for dinner. On the way he told me that he had done very well in the years gone by and was now the head of a flourishing firm similar to the one in India.

He had a cheerful-looking house with a lot of trees and extensive lawns. His fifteen-year-old son was mowing the lawn and had neatly piled up a large quantity of cut grass in a corner. He ought to be watching TV at that hour I thought and not mowing a boring patch of lawn.

When we settled down in the sitting room the young fellow appeared with a tray carrying drinks. He offered us eatables, distributed cigarettes, pushed the side-tables nearer us, arranged the ashtrays and generally took care of us with great courtesy and attention.

While we were discussing old times and remembering our common friends the boy lounged in a sofa at the far end of the room and kept an alert eye on us. At the slightest hint of our needs—whether drinks or cigarettes—he would jump up and bring them to us immediately.

Later, he attended on us at the dining table, served us the dessert and when we finished and went back to the sitting room brought coffee and liqueur. Then, making sure there was nothing more we needed, he took leave of us politely and went in to help his mother clear the table.

I was astonished at this young boy's sense of duty and helpful nature. I expressed my admiration and complimented the father. My friend laughed and said, 'Sure, Jim is helpful; but he is paid to do all this around the house, like tonight. He is a smart guy, though! He has made such a lot of money he has invested it all in stocks! If I don't watch out maybe he will buy up my company one day!'

DARJEELING

MY DECISION to take the train all the way to Darjeeling from Bombay was applauded by everyone as the civilized way to travel when one is on holiday. The Department of Tourism said 'Ah' approvingly and pressed into my hands sheaves of glossy brochures on Ajanta, Varanasi, Darjeeling, Kerala, Mysore, etc. The travel agents who arranged our bookings expressed their delight and viewed me as if I was the first to undertake such a journey by train.

At this point, the train fares were revised and air travel for my wife, son, and me appeared far less expensive. But it was too late to retrace my steps; after receiving a massive approval all round I could not bring myself to go and catch a plane like everybody else.

At Calcutta, my travel agent delivered to me the tickets for our onward journey to Jalpaiguri and wished me bon voyage. 'You will enjoy travelling by the tiny mountain railway from Jalpaiguri to Darjeeling,' announced a friendly ticket collector. 'I am thrilled,' I remarked.

My fellow passengers who seemed to be frequent travellers on that line debated and argued about the time I would have to change over to the mountain train at Jalpaiguri: five minutes, said one, another thought it was thirty minutes, someone else was sure it was only seven minutes.

However, it was a coolie at the other end, half-starved, spindle-legged, looking like a piece of driftwood, who gave the correct information. There was no tiny mountain train going to Darjeeling at all. A disastrous landslide a couple of months earlier had ripped the tracks away! It is still a mystery to me why this vital piece of information was withheld from me, as if by a pact, by everyone concerned with our travel plans.

I could hardly form any impression of the surroundings during the better part of the three hours that it took our taxi to reach Darjeeling. Throughout, the entire landscape was swathed in wads of mist. The driver seemed to depend upon some sense other than vision to keep the car from flying off a cliff or colliding with vehicles madly careering downhill on the narrow road which seemed to have been built for only one car but would, at a pinch, somehow miraculously expand a wee bit to let another coming from the opposite direction pass.

I had watched the unrelieved soupy mist for a couple of hours dully when, all of a sudden, I saw ahead, bathed in the bright sunlight, a refreshing view of a whole mountainside with dark green fir trees and houses neatly stacked one over another. Ah, Darjeeling, at last. So sudden was its appearance it was like some blessed vision. But, alas, it really was: before I could get the full impact of it, it was gone—like a drawing erased by a giant indiarubber leaving the sheet white again. Very soon I could not even see our driver because of the mist between us.

As we drove on, I began to learn that this was the way the eccentric mist behaved. It seemed to take on a personality all its own, quite apart from being just a condition of the general weather. It would let me have a glimpse of the face of a village boy totally abstracted from his surroundings and then reveal nothing for a long time. Then a bit of tree, a hut, goats, all in a blur like an underdeveloped photograph. Then, suddenly, a breathtaking flash of a distant mountain, blue sky, pretty women washing clothes in a waterfall cascading down a cool mountainside. But, again, before I could even realize it, the curtain would go down and the whole drama would cease abruptly.

While I was thus engaged in watching the pranks of the mist, the driver slowed down the car and brought it to a stop. 'This is Tenzing's house, sir,' he proudly pointed out. It was perched at a height, its lawn and flowerbeds sloping down towards the road. Wonderful surroundings to live in for a deserving hero of the mountains, I mused as I watched a man cutting grass in the garden.

Our driver suddenly became all excited and in suppressed delight whispered to me in such a manner that it could have echoed in the valley below, 'That is Mr Tenzing Norgay, sir!'

The grass-cutter immediately turned to us, sharply balancing himself on the sloping patch of grass. His expression seemed uncertain just for a fraction of a second and then his face cracked into a thousand bits, revealing a smile that only Tenzing could flash with such universal warmth and sincerity.

It began to drizzle and, when we reached the government tourist lodge, it was pouring.

The lobby was full of people all dressed up and nowhere to go. They were lounging on the sofa sets looking bored. Our arrival provided a degree of diversion and they surveyed our luggage and stared at us, trying to figure out where we had come from. They all looked like people with names like Basu, Bose, Banerjee, Ghosh, Chatterjee and so on. Later, when I got acquainted with them they indeed had the very names I had guessed!

It was Mr Bose who told me how treacherous the weather had proved; the rains had not ceased since the day he set foot in Darjeeling with his family for a holiday. The others told me they had come to the tourist lodge in driving rain a few days earlier and had remained huddled in their rooms and were returning home the following day, their holiday finished.

'I have already spent a week here, but I have not yet seen Kanchenjunga. If it was not the mist, it was the rain,' wailed Mr Chatterjee. They viewed us with pity as if we had committed an avoidable blunder.

The rain did not stop the whole of that day or that night and sent the mercury hurtling down and our spirits along with it.

But, surprisingly enough, the next morning we saw no trace of cloud, rain or mist. Birds chirruped outside our windows. Trees stood washed and fresh, filling the air with the fragrance of green leaves and wood. Kanchenjunga appeared in dazzling majesty against the blue sky like a cut-out, urging even the most unpoetic minds to respond to its beauty and make silly comparisons to sugar, butter and so forth. A battery of cameras aimed at the snow peaks clicked all round me with the urgency of capturing a fleeting prima donna.

I went for a long walk gulping down the cool mountain air, flushing out the exhaust fumes of the city from my lungs. Everyone I passed on the way seemed to have the same idea. Clusters of families were dashing about in all directions swathed in colourful woollens with a lingering smell of mothballs.

In Darjeeling, wherever one went, the ultimate destination would be the Mall. The Mall is half an acre of flat surface rimmed with park benches on which local beggars and holidaying tycoons relaxed side by side and warmed themselves in the sun. I could sit here for hours on end, lost in observing the goings-on in the middle of the Mall. Young men, pretty girls, Buddhist monks counting the prayer beads while engaged in a lively chat with their companions, pink-cheeked children who were like the winged cherubs by the Old Masters, tired-looking newly-weds on their honeymoon, foreign tourists festooned with cameras, Marwari middle-aged couples grimly taking in their holiday, stout gentlemen having a ride on skinny, undersized ponies.

Then there were pony touts who dressed and behaved like tough cowboys in a Western. The effect however always sadly failed because of their horses which were underfed, mangy and reluctant. The Mall was like a stage. I always went home from here with the sense of having witnessed a play which had a disjointed, fragmentary form, altogether fascinating.

A couple of days later, early one morning, I saw a wisp of white patch tucked away in the valley down below. It began to grow in size rapidly right before my eyes. It was the good old mist returning after a few days of absence. I had almost forgotten its existence. Now, like a mischievous dervish covered with a white flowing beard, it was creeping up the valley to drive the tourists to despair. But luckily we were leaving for Sikkim that day and hoped the dervish would be gone by the time we got back.

It was a fine drive through thickly wooded forests from Darjeeling to Gangtok. Sikkim seemed more advanced than I had thought. The hoardings welcoming the visitors proclaimed breweries, a copper mining corporation and a fruit-juice bottling factory.

In Gangtok, I looked at people's faces trying to imagine them as participants in a mass uprising demanding democratic rights and equal status with India. But I could not: these people seemed cheerfully remote from all that.

I met one of the cabinet ministers of the new government. He tossed out phrases like 'vested interests', 'innocent masses', 'people's aspirations', so expertly with matching expressions and vehement gestures that I might have been listening to a politician anywhere in the world. The Kazi sat next to him with his benign, mysterious smile. The qualities of serenity and composure acquired long ago in a Buddhist monastery as a young man still seemed to survive in him. I could not help wondering how such a man could ever feel at home in politics.

There was a great deal of the old-time atmosphere at the Chogyal's lunch party: the king-size *shamiana* on the palace lawns, royal hospitality in respect of food and drink and to crown it all the palace band playing the tunes of forgotten days. In his immaculate robes the Chogyal was flitting from guest to guest, making his courtesy rounds.

I was taken aback when he came to me and suddenly referred to one of my cartoons showing him in a somewhat awkward situation. His remark was of course friendly. But his smile was rather inscrutable, I felt!

We visited Kalimpong on our way back. It was totally different from what the familiar Tibetan curio shops all over India had somehow led me to expect; semi-dark with a musty smell, ancient streets strewn with copperware and coloured beads. It was none of that. Kalimpong is a neat little town with its shops selling talcum powder, chocolates and baby food.

We came back to Darjeeling for a longer stay. Soon my face became familiar in the Mall and in the bazaar. It was not long before I was actually on grinning terms with the Tibetan carpetseller, the pastrymaker, the girls who knitted sweaters for sale and the photographer who took your picture with Kanchenjunga in the background. As days went by it was becoming increasingly difficult to go on my usual long brisk walks without being stopped every now and then by the local citizenry for friendly gossip.

Going to Tiger Hill is a must when you are in Darjeeling. Here one sees the dawn tint the Himalayan snow ranges pink—an indescribably beautiful view that has made Tiger Hill world-famous. To catch this sight one has to get into a jeep shivering at three in the morning and drive on an unspeakably bad, if not downright dangerous, road to this hill top.

Hundreds of visitors flock to it in season everyday, to stand in the open in freezing cold, their teeth chattering, and wait in hushed silence expectantly for the sun to rise and spray the abstract shapes of clouds with psychedelic hues and fill the yawning vastness around with endless waves of mountains tinged with celestial pink. A wisp of mist could just come in between all these glorious happenings, however, and send the tourist back home disappointed. But we were lucky.

HOLIDAY IN THE ISLANDS

TO START WITH, nobody could tell us how to get there. A few could not even locate the Andaman and Nicobar group of islands on the map. I was even asked why, of all places, I was set on going to these islands. I could not really tell why, but could very well understand the tone of concern in their voice: the old penal settlement in the Andamans perhaps produced an unpleasant association of ideas. So my wife and I were advised to take a trip, instead, to Kashmir or Ooty. But I wanted to visit the islands and approached the government tourist department for guidance. But then I was told that these islands had been grossly neglected by the tourist department and all I would get from them would be their latitude and longitude.

I did not give up: frustration perversely increased my zeal for undertaking the journey. I pressed on madly, asking all and sundry for details and information. After a long time my efforts yielded a letter from a kindly man in Port Blair. I grabbed the opportunity and kept up the communication through a series of letters, telegrams, trunk calls, applications, official form-filling, until we finally hauled ourselves on board the *State of Madras* bound for Port Blair.

I was amazed by the colour of the sea: it was actually a carbon-paper blue. After sailing for four days I saw a small island appear on the horizon faintly, so faint it could have been an illusion, but it caused much excitement all over the ship. Everyone leaned on the railings of the deck to watch it approach ever so slowly and drift by majestically. Other islands of assorted sizes arrived at intervals and departed, all similar with thick mop of vegetation and some with a yellow band of beach skirting them. There are so many islands on the way that the passengers soon lost interest and returned to their paperback horrors and card tables.

There are 350 odd islands in this area which with fascinating names have a ring of romance and mystery about them, as if the names had been given to them by a popular fiction writer: the Labyrinth, Snake, Theresa, Sir Hugh Ross, Harriet, etc. Mercifully they are still out of the reach of our name-changers over here. But for how long? I wonder.

As we drifted towards Chatham to dock, we had a panoramic view of Port Blair. We were shown—as if on a picture postcard—the college building, the Tourist Home, the Naval Institute, the notorious Cellular Jail, which is now regarded as a monument to those who suffered separation and pain behind those grim walls for the sake of our freedom.

Port Blair is a small sleepy town like any on our trunk roads that one drives past without noticing the usual tailoring shop, the hair-cutting saloon, the general stores, the tea shop screaming out music, the bank, the bakery, etc. It even boasts a clock tower and a very clumsily moulded statue of Mahatma Gandhi in a square.

The people here represent nearly every part of India and each one knows at least three languages apart from Hindi, which everyone speaks. There is a refreshing lack of caste consciousness among the people as they mix freely and marry without inhibitions. This broadmindedness is a matter of natural development and not due to the efforts of any social reformer's zeal; paradoxically, in fact, it originated from the promiscuous nature of a sordid penal settlement.

I asked my dhobi how long he had lived in the Andamans. 'I was born here. My grandfather was a convict,' he declared cheerfully. 'He was brought here from Salem. He had chopped off the heads of his sister and her paramour. When released after serving his term, he married a Muslim from Andhra. And my father married a Kerala Christian . . .' This is roughly the standard pattern of anybody's genealogy here, whether he is a shopkeeper, gardener, police official, teacher or political leader.

We took a small boat to the northern islands. The boat chugged on with unhurried grace, sending schools of flying fish rocketing at its approach. One or two sharks made way for us, resentfully brandishing their triangular fins. I was astonished by the colour of the sea. Coral reefs underneath tinted it with fantastic colours ranging from midnight blue to turquoise to the translucent green of emerald in all its purity. However, in a painting, one would have thought this seascape betrayed a poor colour sense on the part of the artist.

The jungles in the islands are impenetrably thick. The trees, gigantic in height and girth, looked as if they belonged more to the world of geology than botany. But for all the awesome appearance, one could easily push one's way through dense undergrowth and make safely for the heart of the forest without fear of attack from wild animals.

We saw no tigers, panthers, jackals or bears in the jungles—in fact no animal other than the deer. But the Jarvas! You are a dead man if they catch you wandering in their territory. They are a tribal people, hostile to anyone who is not a Jarva and they occupy a good part of the western section of the Andamans. Armed with bows and arrows they would attack isolated settlements or road workers on trunk roads. At that time to keep these killers at bay, there was a special police force called the Bush Police deployed throughout the island's jungles at strategic points to keep vigil night and day all the year round.

I was thrilled by the account of the Jarvas and wanted to visit one of the bush police outposts in their region. The police department obliged. We sat precariously balanced in a police canoe and two men padled it through the swamp leading to the interior. One bush policeman sat on the prow with a loaded gun and kept an alert watch on either bank as the boat glided along, gently winding to the left and right to avoid submerged tree stumps, overhanging creepers and mangrove trees. The vegetation got thicker, forming a tunnel, and our course got narrower. Although the sun was shining bright, the thick vegetation gave us a feeling of twilight. Except for the noise of the paddles splashing in the water the silence was absolute. In the narrow, slimy clay bank close by, I suddenly saw a green fat iguana slither into the bushes. It gave me a start: an excusable reaction from a city dweller like me!

The lookout post of the bush police was made of grass thatch on high stilts and its walls of bamboo mats. We took our positions here, surveyed the vast jungle around and waited for the Jarvas. Never had I been to a forest so still and quiet—a strange lack of any jungle noise of animals, birds or insects. The air was surcharged with suspense.

After a long wait I asked the inspector, 'Have you ever seen a Jarva here?' dropping my voice apparently low in deference to the general atmosphere.

'They attacked this outpost only last month. They came up to the edge of the ladder there. Our men here fired and they took to their heels.'

'Did you kill any?' I asked.

He looked at me with horror. 'Certainly not! We have strict orders not to shoot to kill or hurt, but only to scare them away.'

Suddenly my attention was diverted and I saw some movement far away. At once we turned our binoculars to the spot and stared till our eyes popped out. It was some time before we discovered that it was only a spotted deer teaching its young one the trick of vaulting over a bush. It was now time for us to return. And we had not sighted a single Jarva.

As we drifted away in our canoe, I looked back at the receding jungle: the whole atmosphere of the place conveyed to me the Jarvas' dark presence.

Off and on, the local authorities sailed with armed guards with the idea of befriending the hostile tribes and luring them to the mainstream with gifts: plastic buckets, fruits and colourful bits of cloth. But these expeditions always beat a hasty retreat under a shower of arrows. However, I was sure one day the mission would succeed in taming these wild men. I even visualized future visitors beholding them in bush-shirts and trousers, perhaps, with a transistor radio pressed close to the ear. That would be a sad day indeed.

There were a number of tiny islands around Port Blair reachable by boat within a few minutes. Each had an enormous mass of vegetation spread out to the last tip of land, the trees nearly toppling into the sea. Many islands were uninhabited and in some, one saw a forlorn hut or two perched on stilts and dangling a ladder. There were stories, often bloody and dramatic, connected with these islands. Island Harriet, for instance, had a disquieting look and a dilapidated jetty with rusty disintegrating boats moored around it. The Viceroy of India, Lord Mayo, was stabbed to death on this very spot by a convict who had earned freedom for good conduct!

On Viper Island, there was a steep hillock with a curious tumbledown structure on top. The huge pillars, arches and walls suggested that it was part of an ancient palace. But no! This building once sheltered the gallows! My companion, who knew the Andamans inside out and had lived there for many years, explained, 'In those days justice was meted out swiftly, you know,' and proceeded to give a comic sketch of the state of affairs in those days:

'Imagine the British representative on the golf course in far away Port Blair. An officer hurries to the spot to break the news of a murder that has just been committed. His Lordship pauses, listens and asks: "Caught the fellow?"

'"Yes, Sir, we have caught a suspect."

'"What do you mean 'suspect'? He committed it, didn't he? Well, go hang him then."

'Thus, having pronounced the judgement, he gets on with putting the ball. The suspect would be brought here promptly and, of course, hanged!'

Of all the islands, Ross was the most romantic. Except for a couple of rather bored naval security chaps who kept a close watch (on what, I do not know) there was nobody here. But the whole island looked like a movie set straight out of the novels of the Bronte sisters. There were roads, with buildings on either side, office buildings, dance hall, church, playground, bakery, butchery and even a swimming pool complete with a diving board—all signs of gaiety. But alas, all in picturesque ruin! The roofs and walls of the buildings had caved in, the ornate cast-iron gate posts crumpled to the earth, elegant paths swallowed up by hungry vegetation. In the palatial dance hall there was an enormous tree in the middle, its branches pushing through the ceiling and wild creepers squeezing the life out of the supporting beams and pillars.

This island was once the administrative headquarters before the seat of power shifted to Port Blair. In those days the officers, after disposing of the day's work, foregathered here to live it up in true colonial fashion. Liquor flowed copiously in the dance hall and music was heard across the bay till the early hours of the morning by the people in Port Blair. That was the life Ross Island had seen.

I saw a graveyard next to the church in the island. Small but eerie, as dark and gloomy gnarled roots of stunted trees levered up the tombstones. I got closer to examine one of the tombstones which was cracked by roots underneath. It had a sad simple floral border with the inscription: 'John Wood . . . Officer, East India Company Died 1868 Age 23.' The next one belonged to the year 1867 for a person who died at the age of twenty-five. And another, again 1868! The only one resting there who was comparatively old was a captain of a ship who had apparently drowned near Port Blair in 1860 at the age of thirty-five.

We left the Andamans and moved on towards the southern group of islands; Little Andaman, Car Nicobar, Katchal, Komorta, Non Cowry, Theresa down to Camble Bay. Car Nicobar had an individuality all its own. Flat as a table, of its 75 square miles, nearly every other square foot had a coconut tree. A poor man's Hawaii with its blue lagoons and yellow sandy beaches, even the native Nicobary resembles his Hawaiian counterpart in every respect—the physical build, the colour, the ever-present smile down to the flowers around the neck and the colourful sarong.

These islands offered a vast scope for tourist development. There were innumerable beaches, shallow lagoons, pretty coves tucked away in interesting corners, huge solid rocks stuck in the middle of lagoons: I couldn't help visualizing neat little hotels on them. The tourist could jump off right from his window and take a swim, or go yachting or surf-riding or fishing during the season. This part of the world was indeed a paradise on earth.

AUSTRALIA AND I

MY ASSOCIATION with Australia started very early in life. At about the age of three or four I saw a kangaroo in the local zoo. A little later my friends and I became addicted to cricket. We followed the fortunes of the MCC—Marylebone Cricket Club—thinking it was Melbourne Cricket Club and of Australia even before we could understand what the abbreviation stood for. At least one little boy christened his nomadic cricket team the MCC, the Malgudi Cricket Club, after the small town in the south where he lived. Then we collected photographs of Sir Don Bradman, the star of the 'Melbourne Cricket Club', and religiously memorized his score records in various international events and tried out his style and stance with our home-made dealwood cricket bats.

When we grew older, the Australian continent was still with us; in the captivity of our classroom we had to learn all about the Great Barrier Reef, the Blue

Mountains, the boomerang, the emu, the koala bear, the Kalgoorli mines, the duck-billed platypus. Therefore, we'd accumulated a tremendous amount of information about Australia.

And, yet, the whole continent strangely seemed to be floating in grand isolation, far away from our own world.

This sense of remoteness continued even after the Air-India Jumbo put me down at Perth one bright sunny day. In the airport, while I waited for my luggage, the people around me seemed to be going about their business as if in a silent movie. I was struck by the silence around me in such a crowded airport. Driving up to my hotel I saw only motorcars gliding past with the passengers grimly strapped to their seats, and no pedestrians in sight anywhere. Coming from Bombay, the quiet and the absence of crowds in the streets seemed rather strange.

The air in Perth was so pure that I felt my lungs, conditioned to pollution, make quick adjustments with a pleasant tingling sensation. The parks, the bridges, the blue sky, the beaches, the river, the woods—all looked as though they had been put there, based on a blueprint for a picture-postcard.

My Australian friend sitting beside me in the car was reeling off statistics: per capita income, GNP, number of yachts registered and unregistered, population figures, basic wage, etc. But I was strangely deaf to the statistics under the notion, wrong perhaps, that they rather explained away all the magic and left one disenchanted. So, without listening, I sat gazing at a hill-side, awash with wild flowers, the bay below it dotted with flames of multicoloured sails and the cars like strung beads one behind the other rolling up and down the majestic highways laid out neatly between acres and acres of green fields against the background of distant skyscrapers.

At this time the city of Perth was celebrating its antiquity with great gusto. Everywhere one looked one saw neckties, balloons, lapel pins, T-shirts, barrage balloons lolling in the sky, sails of yachts in the bay, not to mention paper bags, napkins and bumper-stickers, all carrying in various sizes a stylized design of a black swan logo symbolizing the occasion. But the city at that time was quite young really, just a hundred and fifty years. It made me feel old; suddenly a silver tumbler at home given to me casually by my mother for drinking coffee came to my mind. It was just as many years old! I gave this bit of news to my companion. He looked at me with an expression as if it were some kind of a museum piece he had been sitting next to and talking!

When meeting an Australian in his own country for the first time one expected a full-blooded American to emerge from under his skin, the slap-happy, flamboyant kind. But no. One found the Australian reserved and soft-spoken with a great capacity to convey his friendliness in a quiet manner. Generally I found him neither loud nor demonstrative, even when the occasion permitted it. For instance, at the races in Melbourne I got a funny feeling looking at the horses dashing towards the winning post neck and neck and the whole crowd watching the event with a silent thrill. The crescendo of goading and urging and the pandemonium that we are so used to were disappointingly missing.

I do not know if there is another nation so devoted to outdoor life as Australia. Nearly everyone I met had a surf-board, a swimming pool and a yacht or two. They played games, watched games, read about games and discussed games. And they also went hiking, mountain-climbing, skiing, fishing, horse-riding, shooting and so on. As if all this were not exhausting enough, a friend I met here who went about playing all these sports religiously took me to his house. After showing me round his big beautiful house with its garden, swimming pool, garage and outhouse, he suddenly asked, 'Like it?' I made appropriate noises.

'I built it,' he declared proudly. I did not immediately realize that he had literally built it with his own bare hands brick by brick! Then he showed me the wooden frame with which he made each brick and explained how he put up the ceiling, laid out the garden, dug the swimming pool and fixed the glazed tiles to its floor, connected the water pipe, installed the water purifier and so on. I was astonished at the man's energy and drive. But there was more surprise in store; he said he did the building job by day and worked in a newspaper office at night!

The people were so busy, engaged in a variety of activties, I hardly noticed anyone talking politics, local or international. Perhaps this was the reason the newspapers here, though bulky, gave short shrift to hard news and seemed eager to get on with ads for consumer goods column after column and page after page. Even the cartoons they carried were thin in political ideas. A well-known political cartoonist has done frontal nude pictures of cabinet ministers. This collection also included Prince Charles wearing nothing but a toothsome royal smile.

Australia was plagued by strikes, I was told; if it was not the postal system which went on strike then it was the transport workers or dock labour. The impression I gathered generally from people was that the unsuccessful trade union leader of Britain had found a haven in Australia for his talents. But I saw no strike drag on painfully. Somehow quick settlements were arrived at and the wheels of industry once again moved, pushing up, of course, wages, taxes and prices, but not yet to a degree, I thought, to give the average citizen reason to worry. Probably, he would turn such a problem into some kind of a novel sport.

I saw evidence of it already. I saw a chap carrying in his car a gadget which looked like a golf stick but with a peculiar head, the size of a saucer. He took it out and operated it and it began emitting a bleeping sound, loud and clear. Seeing the surprised look on my face he said with great excitement, 'A metal detector. I am looking for gold and I am off to the wilderness tomorrow!'

He was not joking. Quite a few indulged in this sport, risking their lives probing and foraging in the old abandoned gold mines and deserted caves in the mountains. I was informed that some were lost forever, not being able to retrace their way, some were flooded and drowned in the mine shafts. There were more than 10,000 Australians engaged in this adventure. I thought the number would be more, considering the profusion of advertisements in the papers offering metal detectors on hire or for outright sale. It all started with one prospector laying his hand accidentally on what looked like just a fair-sized stone but which actually turned out to be 100 per cent gold! He became, of course, a millionaire overnight! The main attraction about such a gold nugget was that the proceeds from the sale of it were totally tax-free, whatever it fetched.

This boundless physical energy of the Australian spending itself out all times, winter, summer and spring, in the sports field, on the snow, under the sea, over the surf, in the sky and so on and on had made it difficult, I thought, for his finer inner qualities to surface. I would have expected that the blue sky, the green fields, the awesome wilderness and the rugged mountains would have made him a poet first and then the great sportsman that he was. I could air my views to my friend freely without the fear of being misunderstood, because I found the Australians generally indulge in self-criticism and analysis very much like the Indian. My critical views were cheerfully shared and approved when I pointed out that their efforts at painting looked very much like those of the Sunday painters of the late nineteenth-century British school.

But eventually they did liberate themselves from the cultural clutches of Europe. New poets and writers have appeared on the scene in the past quarter of a century and their works have been internationally acclaimed. World-renowned painters like Russ Drysdale and Sidney Nolan discovered mystic qualities in the landscape of the desert, the dried and withered trees, even in the dead animals in the drought-stricken regions and typically Australian abstract art blossomed on the canvases of these painters. Sidney Nolan painted a series on the legendary brigand Ned Kelly, who roamed eastern Australia during the latter part of the nineteenth century, dodging the police and the gallows. But in these paintings Nolan created a mythology around Ned Kelly and his life. Somehow I feel it is not necessary to know the depredations of this renegade to appreciate the greatness of Nolan's impressionistic paintings.

Strangely, the poets, singers, painters and writers, go away to live in the United Kingdom or America once they attain success. Perhaps outside Australia they get a feeling of living close to the world of happenings, opportunities, money and fame. Therefore, the custodians of culture in Australia tried to create a bit of such a world in the country itself; they not only encouraged local talent but bought Old Masters at fabulous prices. At the time I was in Australia, they acquired a painting of Jackson Pollock paying millions of dollars and also invited Russian ballet, European opera, Indian music and classical dance troupes to perform at their prestigious Sydney Opera House, the architecture of which has caused much controversy. I could well understand the reason the moment I beheld it.

Its outside appearance shrieked for attention as if that was an end in itself. I was shown this building with the flourish of introducing me to some kind of a puzzle which could reveal many artistic delights once you got the hang of it. I did not even know where to begin to unravel it to get at all those treasures. Luckily, the girl who herded the tourists on a conducted tour of the building explained how to appreciate, what to admire, how to gasp in artistic ecstasy, marvel, and so on. Still, in my view, the architecture did not even fit into its surroundings, the weather-beaten buildings, the old bridge, the river and the boats. This disharmony itself was described to me as a vital point of great

artistic merit. Luckily its interior was sober and conventional like any opera house. This building, I thought, symbolized the young nation's urge to shock for the sake of getting instant cultural recognition.

Like elsewhere, the immigrants from Italy, Greece, India, Yugoslavia and Turkey who have settled here for more than a couple of generations frequently return to the land of their origin and bring back a bit of the outside world, good and bad. I saw Italian restaurants, Chinese tea houses, Indian yoga centres . . . And one day resting my limbs in Melbourne sitting on a park bench I suddenly even heard the approaching sound of a harmonium. It was soon followed by the strong smell of incense sticks. Sure enough along came a Hare Krishna group, clapping, dancing and singing away in praise of the Lord as if it was in Chowpatty.

On the last day in Australia, waiting in my hotel lobby for the car to take me to the airport, I was casually turning over in my mind the experiences of my travel. An old man sitting next to me examined the tag on my luggage, smiled and asked, 'Come from India?' His dress was pretty rumpled, fingernails chipped, and chin unshaven. 'Going to,' I replied.

'I just returned from there.' He volunteered the information and a dialogue ensued. He was a millionaire, one of those who kept a sheep farm. But he had retired and was lonely, his wife having died long ago. Now his children and grandchildren took care of his business and he spent his time travelling. 'I spent eight months travelling all over India: Sikkim, Bangalore, Taj Mahal, Tiruchirapalli, Madurai, Jaipur, Cuttack, Nagercoil . . .' He would have gone on but my car had arrived and I left with my opinion of Australia as a continent floating away in remote isolation drastically changed.

MAURITIUS

THE WORLD ATLAS I have with me has many little dots and specks which have really nothing to do with the world or geography. It is an old one, and time, the weather and generations of cockroaches have put them there. So it was with some difficulty that I was able to locate Mauritius in the vastness of the Indian Ocean. It is a tiny speck of an island situated below the Equator on the twentieth parallel some 4,500 km south-west of Bombay.

Our aircraft is bearing us towards it. Through the occasional rent in the clouds I glimpse the ocean spread like a bluish-grey sheet of steel. There are acres and acres of cloud below me having all sorts of funny shapes in an odd abstract way. Curiously they resemble figures in the ancient legends of China, Rome, Greece, India and what-have-you.

I have several hours yet to pass and so I engage myself in this fascinating business of creating cloud-sculptures. I see the rippling muscles of Atlas, or was it Hercules? An enormous coiled cobra with Vishnu, I think, reposes tranquilly in the middle. The whole piece also suggests a profile of some divinity or other but at the moment is rapidly dissolving to take on the form of a Chinese dragon. There are several Spanish galleons, elephants and flocks of woolly sheep . . . The hum of the aircraft changes. The loudspeaker crackles. We fasten our seat belts and land in Mauritius.

I cannot help drawing a comparison, albeit ridiculous and rather far-fetched, between my vague observations at 10,000 metres watching the clouds and what I learn of Mauritius later. This tiny island has an astonishingly similar variety, strange juxtapositions, incongruities, odd mixtures of race and language.

Here Africans and Chinese, Biharis and Dutch, Persians and Tamils, Arabs, French and English all rub shoulders merrily with one another and emerge with a peculiar sense of oneness. A Tamil, for instance, bears a deceptively south Indian face and a name to go with it to boot; Radha Krishna Govindan is indeed from Madras. I speak to him in Tamil. He surprises me by responding in a frightfully mangled English with a heavy French accent. Mr Govindan has no knowledge of Tamil and his tongue has ceased curling to produce Tamil sounds centuries ago!

Like several of his fellow men, his ancestors were brought to the islands as slaves or, later, as indentured labourers to work in sugarcane fields and factories or to cut timber in the jungle and haul it to the boats.

Their roots in their original homelands withered and disappeared with the passage of time. All of them happily came to share in the triumphs and defeats of whoever happened to be their masters among the buccaneering trinity of those days—the Dutch, the French and the English who constantly waged battles for the possession of the island for its spices and sugar or just for the strategic position on the maritime route to the East, conveniently placed as it was for piratical purposes.

However, the battle of 1810 ended all that in favour of the English. The French surrendered and handed over the island after extracting a favour from the conquerors that the French influence on the island be left intact. The English kept their word to the last day of their rule, which ended in 1968. And so we still have very musical but unpronounceable names in Mauritius like Trouaux Biches, Beau Bassin, Quarter Bornes, Curepipe, Ross Belle and so on.

The government at the time conducted all its affairs in English, probably carried on unofficial discussions in French and undoubtedly thought in Creole, a dialect which contains a bit of everything: French, Persian, African, Malay, Arabic, Tamil, Hindi, Chinese, English, etc. I was told that the Tamil *Ai-aiyyo*—a very spontaneous all-purpose expression of unpleasant surprise—is in common usage in Creole! But the people, however, retained their separate religious identities. There were quite a few mosques, churches, temples, and Chinese pagodas. Yet religious clashes and tensions were quite unknown at the time.

The people seemed extremely relaxed and warm towards strangers. In the streets, in the bazaar, in restaurants, it was common to be greeted and smiled at as if you were a long-lost friend. Coming from Bombay, with my fixed grim expression of a city-dweller, I reacted awkwardly at first to such spontaneity and felt ashamed that I wasn't even able to manage a smile.

The same atmosphere of friendliness prevailed even in Port Louis, the seat of government. The cabinet ministers and others in high positions didn't act as if they were born to the grace. They seemed just like ordinary people one bumps into in an airport lounge or in a hotel lobby. They were unassuming, accessible, communicative and, above all, went about without a protective shield of hangers-on and security men to repel casual approaches. I was shown a modest-looking flat in a busy street lined with shops and crawling traffic: the residence of the prime minister of Mauritius.

Port Louis brought to my mind Joseph Conrad and Somerset Maugham. The little port town seemed as if it was built at the suggestion of these writers to suit their novels and short stories. Merchant ships, trawlers, dinghies stood anchored in the harbour with cobwebs of ropes and festoons of flags hanging from their masts. Grimy sailors and dockhands in seamen's caps lounged on oil drums and packing cases or leaned against bleak warehouse walls, smoking pipes.

Facing the harbour a few hundred metres away I spotted a statue, of the founder of Mauritius, Mahe de la Bombdonnais, in wig, breeches and frock-coat. Far away behind him, hidden by graceful queen palms and gulmohur trees, stood one of the most beautiful colonial buildings on the island. This was the Government House.

Sugarcane fields like a carpet of green covered the island on all sides as far as the eye could travel up to the foot of the distant blue mountains that formed a ring around the island—a volcanic happening of geological ages. These mountains do not have the traditional monotonous pyramidal shapes. Their outlines are freakish and whimsical with unexpected sweeps and perpendicular drops and pin-pointed peaks precariously doing a balancing act with boulders as big as a skyscraper!

There is no railway in Mauritius. Well-maintained trunk and arterial roads connect various villages and towns, cutting through the ubiquitous sugarcane fields. Although the whole country is only 64 km by 50 km in size, driving round the island for sight-seeing made me feel curiously as if I was in a place as sprawling as India. But the excellent weather and breathtaking landscapes all around made up for the many hours spent just sitting inside a car. It is very common for people here to drive up and down an average 70 km to a cocktail party or dinner with friends.

The trees in Mauritius were unlike the gigantic specimens I saw in the Andaman Islands. Disappointingly enough, they were short and gnarled even in the interior of jungles, looking like abnormally

overgrown bonsai. Furthermore, the jungles had no wildlife, not even poisonous snakes or insects. The bat was the only mammal before man arrived on the island with the monkey and the deer centuries ago. Unfortunately even the birds were dwindling in number and variety. The dodo, a bird which could not fly and which certainly had no claims to beauty and elegance, a native of this island is extinct now. And so are the giant tortoises of the Aldabra variety, of which a few specimens have been brought and kept in an enclosure in the botanical gardens at Pomplemousses.

What intrigued me wherever I went even in the well-tended botanical gardens, were a colossal number of trees uprooted and lying on the ground in all directions, drying in the sun to become faggots. I saw a whole valley full of trees, thousands of them, bleached to the colour of bone, twisted and scattered about like giant toothpicks spilled out of their containers.

However, despite amazing natural beauty, the island had also had its share of natural disasters. The people of Mauritius could never forget the night the King cyclone struck them. On 6 February, 1975, a 320-km-broad howling wind moved in at some 255 km per hour. The eye of the cyclone alone, I was told, was 48 km wide and it churned the country for two days, relentlessly flattening everything that stood, smashing windows and doors, tearing up roof tops, uprooting trees and bringing them down on buildings.

The island of course recovered from the devastation. But the valley of dead trees gave me a fair idea of the enormous violence the cyclone had wreaked on these people, who were actually quite used to facing these storms as they are an annual event in Mauritius. But the big ones come only once in fifteen years. Like most tragedies however, by the time the next one is due the memory of the previous disaster fades or merely comes a myth. So, again, trees are planted in congested areas, tall buildings come up, plateglass picture windows are fixed and roof tops are put up with an eye on elegance. But, sure enough, at the end of the fifteen-year period, the King cyclone appears promptly on the horizon to surprise the people of Mauritius.

A coral reef runs all around the island parallel to the shoreline, keeping the hysterical waves away at a safe distance from the beaches. The calm turquoise-blue lagoons of Mauritius have thus become world-famous. They are still and calm like lotus ponds and are a delight to those who like water sports such as scuba-diving, swimming, surf-riding, speedboat racing, and yachting. In some places the sea is so shallow there is even horse-riding.

My wife and I not being aquatic, watched with amusement the avidity of the tourists from all parts of the world extracting every bit of fun that the magnificent beach could yield.

We decided to go on a cruise to see coral reefs and marine life and were taken on a boat with a glass bottom. There were seashells on yellow sands to start with: little undefinable creatures, stray bits of seaweed floated by. Alarmed crabs scurried for shelter. Then came the skeleton-like formation of coral. The sea deepened; pale green bushes, slimy white blobs big as pumpkins, lobsters, slithering snaky forms.

As the glass-bottomed boat moved further into the sea the scene below turned eerie; among the jagged rocks the coral jungle became dense and huge and was draped with a brownish moss. I saw shapeless ugly creatures crawling in the dark depths of the sea; I felt unblinking eyes watching us from below the giant mushroom-like growth all over; headless animals pretending to be plants, stuck in one place, swayed from side to side in a ghostly manner. A cold shiver ran down my spine.

All of a sudden, standing out against the darkness, a school of fish—coloured bright lemon-yellow with black bars all along their sides—passed majestically by, cheering up the whole world of overwhelming gloom. Further on I saw the coral branches tipped with a peculiar blue light like hundreds of candles dying out; plenty of colours appeared now: violet, yellow, pink, green, postbox red. Fishes with hideous spikes all over their body, fishes with long tails, fishes with battered faces, all of them with the damned look of condemned souls, criss-crossed our path in a weird twilight against a nightmarish landscape.

Again something appeared to relieve the gloom; a patch of what looked like a lilac garden with each flower having a dash of yellow most beautifully in the middle. But I was cautioned; these were really creatures capable of causing deadly harm to the trespasser! Familiar objects began to appear again, algae, shells, a Kleenex tissue carton! I thank my lucky stars I am not a fish!

While fastening my seat belt on my return flight I vaguely thought of the future of Mauritius. Will it be able to preserve its pristine charm? It had no population problem with its 8,50,000 people evenly spread out all over the country. There was hardly any unemployment as people seemed to live fairly well at all levels. The government seemed aware of all these advantages but felt a certain nervousness about an economy completely dependent on a single commodity—sugar. Logically therefore it was eager that foreign entrepreneurs start their industries here.

I conjured up the rest of the scenario. With industrial growth, the living space will shrink. Cars and trucks will increase. Roads will have to be widened to take the load. The price of land will go up and flats will appear. Cost of living, pollution, unemployment, slums, taxation, controls . . . However, an enlightened people can, of course, guide themselves away from all such evils and still preserve this paradise on earth.

I turned hopefully to the window for the clouds to entertain me. But the sun had set. It was dark outside and I would be in India in a few hours.

IMPRESSIONS OF KATHMANDU

A SMALL KNOT OF PEOPLE drowsily watched the incoming passengers at Kathmandu airport. As I looked at them, my heart sank, for my friend was not among them. Before coming here, friends and well-wishers had given me a welter of contradictory advice and information: that it would be hot in Nepal, that it would be cold; that there was no need for a passport, that I had to have a passport or I would be thrown out; that the Customs would harass me, that the Customs officials were gentle and hospitable; and that I would get hepatitis the moment I landed.

I had not bothered to sort out which was right and which wasn't, hoping to entrust myself entirely to the care of my friend the moment I alighted from the plane and have a holiday which was both safe and enjoyable. Now I panicked as he had not come to take care of me and get me through Passport, Health, Immigration, and Customs without complications.

Inside the airport, I was further perturbed. Near the passport section I heard the plaintive voice of an old American lady pleading, 'But, officer, I was definitely assured that there was no need for a visa for Nepal . . .'

The glare outside was more fierce than the sun. The airport coach lumbered slowly towards the city through a neatly sectioned carpet of lush green paddy fields. I sat back comfortably in my seat to enjoy the scenery. Far away, the mountains looked like tents in several shades of blue. But just as I was about to become poetic, dismal, ramshackle huts appeared and spoilt my mood. They huddled around brown stagnant ponds in which women were washing clothes and vessels, collecting water in pots and carrying them into their huts. A very familiar sight for one coming from India. But why here, of all places, I thought. Half a dozen rivers originate in the Himalayas and it seemed ironical that these people should depend on stagnant pools!

I was roused from my sombre musings as a huge structure in concrete and steel aggressively came into view. It looked patently like a foreign-aid project trying to push a developing country towards modernization and better living.

As soon as we entered the city, an enormous playground monopolized the attention of everyone in the coach. An important-looking cricket match was feverishly in progress. I felt curiously disappointed at this sight; I expected to see something out of the ordinary, something unique and romantic, and cricket came as an anti-climax. As if that were not enough, there were huge hoardings all over the place, irritatingly familiar, advertising radios, biscuits and cigarettes. I could have been in one of the minor suburbs of Bombay!

I guess I was being too hasty in my judgement because a mile away from the hoardings, the cricket and the cars, I discovered the slumbering ancient world. The streets here dating back to the fifth century, were cobbled, very narrow and dark except for a ribbon of sunlight woven out of shimmering dust and a million swarming flies. The houses on either side were real antiques which an American collector would have taken away and placed in his drawing room, if he could. I felt that if I looked at them hard enough they would crumble into a heap of dust. In reality, they were quite sturdy, built of brick and wood, and seemed to have withstood beatings from the weather and from invaders, for centuries.

The wooden doors and windows of even the tiniest houses bore rich carvings of Vishnu, Shiva, Buddha, grimacing dragons, snakes, mythical birds, ornate flowers and often erotic themes. The artistic exuberance of the decoration contrasted oddly with the dwellers, who looked pathetically poor and humble.

At my approach, faces appeared, framed expensively in the doorways and windows. Their eyes fluttered in warm friendliness and their features were delicately set; I felt that the Nepalese faces were capable of no other expression except a perpetual smile.

The people of the Himalayan Kingdom are unbelievably attractive. All the women looked like rugged beauties, carefully dressed and painstakingly made up for a movie shooting. Children, in the pink of health, shabbily dressed, their faces and hands smeared with dirt, rolled playfully with the ubiquitous mangy, pink mongrels, shouting, laughing and darting about like sparrows.

Their charm and physical well-being seemed beyond the reach of any disease. Looking at them, I nearly lost faith in the accepted notions of hygiene and medical precautions.

The cobbled lane led me to an open square ahead. Till I actually entered it I couldn't guess its vastness. It was surrounded on all sides by innumerable temples and palaces of gigantic proportion. And so were the bronze bells, drums, stone lions, rhinos and carved pillars that cluttered the entire square. I stood dwarfed in amazement and wondered which mediaeval giant built this city, and am told that the entire city is in the courtyard.

Soon I discover him, or rather his statue in bronze, perched on a tall bronze pillar genuflecting in all humility before the entrance to the temple of Shiva which he built.

I think he had great foresight in believing in vast spaces for the survival of his glory: it would otherwise have perished without trace as several vegetable sellers, fishmongers and innumerable other vendors took over the place subsequently. They were everywhere, on the temple steps and up to the feet of the God. Dogs, of course, followed them, foraging for food. Monkeys roamed about on an equal footing with the men and seemed to stop just short of transacting actual business.

I was tickled to see a grassseller who having stuffed bundles of grass into the open mouth of a ferocious angry stone lion was comfortably reclining against its huge powerful paws. My attention was drawn to a tourist guide going on his appointed round meekly followed by dumbstruck tourists. They clicked away with their cameras greedily as if the vision in front of them would vanish in another minute. Just then I almost tripped over the outstretched legs of a hippie sitting on the ground. He and his flower-consort were reclining against a stone wall which enclosed an ornate fountain, now of course bone dry, serving as a pen for a goat seller's capricious flock.

The hippies wore the usual beads, Buddha medallions and mystic symbols of Tibet embossed on copper plates. They cuddled each other and gazed on the bustle and activity around them dispassionately. The far-away look is, however, merely the result of

dope which is freely available and has made Nepal a haven for hippies.

On the horizon far away I see faint chalk scribblings; snow peaks of the distant Himalayas. At this time of the year they usually remain concealed under a thick blanket of haze. To see them better I have to take a trip to a mountain top early in the morning and await the dawn and take my chance. So I hurry back to my hotel to make arrangements for a car to take me to the mountains next day.

It is evening and all the shops are brightly lit in the main shopping centre of the city. Foreign tourists are flocking into the antique shops. I hear an European lady ask one of the shopkeepers, 'This is Buddha. Yes?' I look at the foot-high bronze image she is pointing to in the showcase. It is the goddess Tara sitting in the classical pose on a lotus, stripped to the waist. I suppress my laughter and go on to see what the other shops are selling.

They are all chock-full of imported goods: transistors, tape-recorders, cosmetics and cameras and, of course, crowded with tourists from India.

'Do you like Nepal?' asks one of my countrymen.

'Yes, very much,' I reply.

'Been to the casinos and night clubs?'

'No, I have no time for them.

'No time? Then what do you do in a place like this?'

Sketches

REMINISCENCES ON THE 1942 STRUGGLE

My IMPRESSIONS of our freedom struggle in 1942 are from a sick bed in my hometown in Mysore. I was fighting a battle of my own—a battle for survival, having caught a virulent type of typhoid fever about the time Mahatma Gandhi gave the Quit India call.

One day when I hazily saw my mother peering anxiously at me, I realized that it had been more than thirty days since I had last seen her. During all that time I had been almost unconscious and only that morning did I show some hopeful signs of recovery!

In time I got better and was soon able to pick up news titbits about the world outside, from conversations with visitors who sat and chatted around my bed. I learnt that schools and colleges were closed and that students were eagerly participating in the fight to rid the country of British rule.

I was told that one of my closet friends had been arrested and imprisoned. I was shocked! He was a soft-spoken, mild and frail chap without a trace of aggressiveness. From kindergarten to college we had sat side by side, listening to the lectures in various classrooms, exchanging innocent jokes and comments. Now, the news of his arrest really gave me a physical jolt.

He had joined what was known as the 'Cycle Brigade' which simply meant going all over the town on bicycles shouting anti-British slogans. In the beginning the police, who had no bicycles to give effective chase, found it difficult to apprehend them. Finally they tricked the 'Brigade' into a lane, threw a rope across it and hauled the catch off to prison!

Some days later my friend sent me a grubby-looking postcard from prison. Two black bars censored some matter in it which the jail superintendent evidently considered offensive to His Majesty the King of England. The rest, the uncensored bits on the card, were all about the poor standard of the prison library!

A little later another card arrived. This time my friend wrote that the inmates were fed on soup prepared out of grass and that the rice smelt of phenyl.

Gradually, disquieting news about conditions in the prison and the treatment of the prisoners began trickling in frequently. There was talk of prison unrest and rioting, and soon everybody had heard about the boy who had died with boot marks on his chest.

Yet throughout the period of upheaval the police force remained rigidly loyal to the British. That was, of course, understandable: after all, they were paid to keep their masters' idea of law and order. But what was deplorable was the wanton brutality they seemed to revel in while carrying out their duty. Even nice chaps in the service, normally known for their ready, friendly smiles and pleasant natures, became instantly beastly as if transformed by an ugly witch.

Our next-door neighbour was a chubby-looking police inspector who greeted everyone warmly, took his children to the park, and would bargain even with the vegetable vendor with a kind of winning humour and understanding. But during the days of the crisis he quickly earned a reputation: that of a mini-Hitler! The visitors at my bedside described with horror the manner in which he swung his baton and gleefully brought it down on the demonstrators, cracking the skulls of his friends and of the sons of his friends!

More mystifying was the behaviour of the city magistrate whom we used to look upon with respect and a certain admiration. He was a man with an extremely affable nature and a philosophical turn of mind who carried himself with a dignity becoming of his qualities and attainments. This man who also must have panicked at the sight of a slogan-shouting mob gave orders to open fire which led to the death of a college student. Of course, later the magistrate justified his action to us with all the intellectual objectivity and philosophic reasoning he could muster.

In course of time a prominent circle in one of the main thoroughfares in Mysore was named after the young man who died in police firing. We hope our friend, the magistrate, perhaps felt a twinge of guilt and awkwardness whenever he passed that way to reach his office.

Though these stories aggravated the gloom in the sick room, yet occasionally one heard of events which were downright comic. For instance, there was this person belonging to the senior section of our college; an intelligent man; he sincerely believed, of all things, that the British were ultimately going to stay on in this country! This notion indeed put him in many odd situations. He paid a couple of visits to my bedside and I nearly split my sides listening to his crazy views on our efforts to get freedom from the British. This diversion resulted in my having a relapse; I had exerted too much, the doctor said, laughing.

He became increasingly pro-British with the passing of each day. His cocky stance of an adversary constantly led to fierce arguments which luckily for him stopped just short of an exchange of blows. But he could not enjoy this kind of restraint on the part of his friends for long.

Labouring under a false idea of being intellectually honest at a time when some down-to-earth common sense was needed, he began to get tactlessly bolder and louder in airing his views. In his gait, manners and accent he started modelling himself carefully after the image of the English professors and lecturers in our university. The delusion was so complete that one day he referred to Mahatma Gandhi as 'Mr Gandhi' with the spontaneity of Colonel Blimp. But soon after uttering that, the poor man had to flee the spot as those who heard him were now after his blood. He took refuge in one of the quarters belonging to a professor of English. There he remained, not venturing out throughout the period of the crisis, learning Milton and Macaulay at first hand from the professor. In fact, when normalcy was restored and exams resumed, he stood first in English literature!

By and large the students who fought for Independence showed admirable grit and tenacity in pursuing their objective and facing police brutality. One of them particularly won my unqualified admiration as I heard about his exploits day after day. He had a peculiar air of casual boldness while doing even simple deeds. He became the natural leader of the student movement in 1942. While addressing public meetings, when he was prohibited from doing so, he sang patriotic songs in front of police barracks, asked his followers to disobey all police orders: and all this was done without theatrical gestures or delirious speeches. Perhaps even the police found it hard to hit or shout at such a man although, of course, he was marched off to the prison many a time.

Once, when he was released after the authorities made sure it would be safe to do so, he did precisely what they had warned him not to and was whisked off to jail again, this time for a prolonged spell. After his release, he immediately dragged a huge temple chariot, with the help of his follower, into the middle of a busy road and blocked all traffic for hours. As expected, he was escorted back to his cell to serve his sentence for the many breaches of law that this one act had caused.

Gradually the situation vis-a-vis the freedom struggle returned to normal. It took nearly a year for me to get back to college. There I noticed that the number of professors from England had dwindled and also that the brave freedom fighters of yesteryears were subdued and worried about the approaching exams and the future. Anyway, all of them passed out of college and disappeared into the wide world, looking for jobs. I have lost track of most of them. Recently, I searched the list of '*Thamra Pathra*' recipients hoping to find one familiar name, but in vain.

However, a few who I still keep in touch with and who had distinguished themselves in the past as heroes, are now well settled in good jobs, either heading important government departments or occupying swivel chairs as executives managing big commercial business enterprises. A couple of them who I had the honour of knowing in those days became cabinet ministers too. And even the one who threw in his lot with the British during the freedom struggle, today not only holds a prestigious position but his advice is sought on matters of national importance; he also belongs to a very busy seminar circuit.

THE UGLY POLITICIAN

THE SITUATION in the country has become so hilarious that the dividing line between the caricature and the caricatured has almost disappeared. Alarmingly, the politicians walk, talk and behave as though they are modelling perpetually for the cartoonist. Who knows, perhaps cartoons do exercise some sort of subtle influence on their manners and even looks, reducing them to the cardboard characters they have become in real life.

People curious about my work often ask me how I get the ideas for my cartoons. My reply usually is that the politicians work for me—or something on those frivolous lines.

Somehow, the word 'politician' has come to mean anything but what he fancies himself to be: someone wise, dignified and dedicated. On the other hand, the image that actually forms in our mind is that of a somewhat pompous, comical figure more like the character in a cartoon.

These qualities get magnified if the politician happens to be a successful one and a minister. In this role he really sweats to keep the cartoonist ceaselessly busy. The unsuccessful ones keep themselves active by holding demonstrations in front of ministers' houses and offices shouting angry slogans, burning the effigies of men in power, going on indefinite fasts (unfortunately they are never for more than a couple of days at a stretch), *gheraoing* unprotected individuals, etc.

All this is carried out, of course, to eliminate the ills in our system and bring justice to the common man. Further, they also know various other ways to hold back inflationary prices, overcome shortages of essential commodities and correct defective demarcations of their state borders. These involve smashing railway carriages, reducing buses to ashes, organizing bandhs and stoning restaurants. Such behaviour might look suspiciously like the pathetic results of deep frustration. But no; we are told it is politics at work in a true democracy.

Since this style of opposition to the establishment has to be largely conducted under the open skies, it could be quite a trying business, especially if age and the elements are against one, as it often happens. Naturally, temptation grows steadily stronger under such conditions to defect to the tantalizing side of the rulers; there the defector always has a good chance of being received hospitably and given a berth in the

Cabinet. From there he could carry out the onerous task of removing poverty and misery sitting on a plush chair in air-conditioned comfort without being baked in the sun or getting soaked in the rain.

But, unfortunately, not all defections lead to ministership. Invisible pressures of caste, groupism, parochialism and just ordinary favouritism might stand in the way of an innocent defector becoming even a deputy minister. In such a case, he hastily does a right or left about-turn and sets about to work assiduously towards toppling the government with the hope of heading it himself. Often the tactics pay off and he starts enjoying the fruits of office till such time as he himself is toppled. As it is rather inconvenient to be thrown out of power every other day the risk is usually mitigated by the potential troublemaker being absorbed into the Cabinet quickly—and thus pleasantly silenced. But this has become very much like the attempts of a drowning man, who tries to gulp down the ocean to keep himself afloat.

Come to think of it, there is no opposition party in this country, really! Those at the Centre seem to preserve their 'enemies' just to project to the world the picture of a fair-minded democratic system. That is why I always find it more fun to concentrate on people in power. They are more exposed, vulnerable, commit uproarious blunders and unabashedly get involved in scams from which they emerge cheerfully unscathed.

People enjoy seeing such antics of the ministers caricatured because they get a vicarious kick out of hypocrisy and pomp ridiculed, ego punctured.

In the early days of our Independence I was filled with tremendous hopes like everyone else for the future. Having relentlessly attacked the foreign rulers and packed them off finally, I saw, suddenly, a whole nation free from all social injustices, economic disparities, police brutality, protests and violence. I decided to treat our own men at the helm of affairs with reverence and understanding. So, while they were engaged in various nation-building activities, I settled down with my brush to help our leaders in their tasks.

I was young. Jawaharlal Nehru, of course, was my hero. While drawing I began to bestow care on him at the risk of even sacrificing the element of satire which is the soul of the art of caricature. I used to make his lower lip less protruding in my cartoons, gave height to his stature, put the white cap at a jaunty angle and nearly succeeded in making him look a combination of Captain Marvel and Superman of comics fame. Thus I armed him to face boldly the gigantic challenges of our economic, social, political and linguistic problems of the post-Independence times. All went well for a few months.

But gradually I began to sense the satirist in me stirring uneasily every time I saw my own cartoons in the paper whose headlines and columns screamed for an altogether different kind of reaction from the cartoonist. Nehru's policies and utterances seemed incongruous with the saviour's image I was trying to cast him in. The business of preserving his image, pampered and glorified, began to be embarrassingly tough. So I liberated myself one day by throwing away his famous cap and exposing his bald pate with its fringe of white hair. To his figure I added a little paunch too and, above all, became deeply indebted to him for becoming one of the staunch suppliers of ideas for me during his time.

After the transformation of Nehru, others slid effortlessly into their places to serve me: K.M. Munshi, G.L. Nanda, Jagjivan Ram, S.K. Patil, R.A. Kidwai, etc. Particular mention here must be made of Morarji Desai and V.K. Krishna Menon for sparing no effort to help me gain some modest success and popularity in my career.

I have often wondered why ministers look the way they do—as if they belonged to a totally different species. Luckily, I had an opportunity to examine this phenomenon at close quarters. I was a witness to the actual transformation of an ordinary, simple sort of a fellow into a minister. To the surprise, shock and despair, variously, of all who knew him, a friend of mine, a quiet, self-effacing man, became a minister.

The very first change which was conspicuous after becoming a minister was his acquiring enormous wealth within record time. He went about his business surrounding himself with a mob of like-minded people and became quite inaccessible even to his old friends. Nevertheless, he kept in touch with the masses through his photographs in the dailies and through loudspeakers from which his voice blared from the Olympian heights of decorated platforms on which he was found at public functions day after day. The range of subjects this erstwhile jaggery merchant could hold forth on at such gatherings astonished me. He would speak with a ring of authority in his voice on subjects varying from the virtues of salted biscuits to the vulnerability of the Indian Ocean to foreign domination, from the need to remove poverty and kick the capitalist in the pants to Bharatanatyam, fertilizer and the threat of the CIA. No matter what the subject of his speech, he always managed to convey the impression at the end that he had been disappointed with the people for not sacrificing enough for the country besides frustrating his own efforts to take the nation to its salvation.

Even his appearance changed. He became comfortably rotund and his starched cap and jacket gave him an air of superiority which began to seem misleadingly real. His eyes, which had an innocent charm and honesty in his pre-ministerial days, now remained fixed thoughtfully on the row of glittering coat buttons resting on his paunch. He was at the height of his career at this time: he looked extraordinarily prosperous, invincible, triumphant and powerful, like a conqueror. And even I, a cynical fellow, could not help but feel a twinge of inferiority in his presence.

However, fate struck! There was a Cabinet reshuffle because of the usual petty infighting and my friend was unceremoniously dropped. It was shocking to see him literally reel under the impact of the news and suddenly shed all appearances and roll on his expensive carpet bemoaning his fate. Through tear-drenched eyes he looked at the few of us who had gathered around him and told us with touching sincerity what a wonderful man he really was and what bloody crooks his colleagues were who were still ministers nibbling away at the opportunity to make money and more money. He held out dark threats that one day he would indeed expose the chief minister himself whom he said he had served loyally till then.

After ranting thus for hours, he finally recovered from the blow and cheerfully declared that he was indeed happy he was out of the Cabinet and that he looked forward to living like a free man without the worries and responsibilities of a minister. He confided to me that he had modest means to support himself and his family: two cinema theatres leased out, a three-star hotel, four bungalows rented to foreign companies in his wife's name and a few other sources of income.

'You look so happy now! Supposing you are included in the second list tomorrow? Would you turn down the offer or would you sacrifice your happiness and accept a Cabinet post?' I asked.

He seemed confused for a moment. 'Ah, you cannot put it that way. I will serve my country in whatever capacity I am asked to,' he replied with a deep expression of humility, pressing his palms together humbly. That moment he was a cartoon personified!

By and large this is the stuff the species called the minister is made of. He wants to be a minister as long as he lives. He will not step down from office under any circumstances. If, occasionally, a minister is forced to retire because of age or political expediency, you will find him biding his time in the wings exerting subtle pressures ranging from abject appeal to open blackmail to get into the Cabinet again. In extreme cases, of course, erring, irresponsible ministers are got rid of by appointing them governors of states.

All this I view with a sense of humour as politicians provide abundant grist to the cartoonist's mill. But there are moments when I panic: the way things are getting I fear the day is not far off when politicians will do the cartoonist out of his job by taking over the business of making people laugh directly or more likely, through a corporation.

I can hear, at this point, the ministers protesting and saying that this is just another instance of exaggeration and misreporting by the press. I can imagine them following it up with an official denial somewhat to the effect that 'the Government has no plans to amuse the public directly and that it would continue to do so only through the medium of the cartoonist'.

'HOW I DID IT!'

AT SCHOOL I copied 'Jack and Jill' in the exam from a three-year-old girl seated next to me and got promoted. At the age of seven, or maybe eight, one day I nervously pocketed the balance of a rupee after buying a packet of cigarettes for my absent-minded father. I continued to do so until the time I was old enough to qualify for the legitimate monthly allowance.

Then, with the help of lime, paraffin oil and soap, I began to conduct messy experiments in our kitchen on used postage stamps to give them a second lease of life. After many frustrating attempts I nearly succeeded with one of them which had escaped official cancellation with barely visible marks. After my treatment it really looked as good as new and my joy knew no bounds that day. The money I would be making through this discovery of mine seemed almost limitless. But my dream was never fulfilled: I never used this stamp. After all the labour I spent on it I could not summon the little courage that was needed to cheat His Majesty's Government even though it would not have been more than a few coppers. I gave up the stamp business.

This slight cowardice led me away from more daring ventures like trying to make counterfeit coins and spurious drugs.

However, at a later stage, I felt no fear of any sort when I launched out on my next project. I began to supply a local magazine in our town with short stories pilfered from an obscure book in an old Hungarian collection.

The plot and other aspects of those stories delighted the editor and the readers. Of course, to avoid detection of their source, I localized them thoroughly by disguising the characters and the Hungarian setting. In course of time I flourished as a writer this became such a routine job that I became lazy and hardly bothered to hide the Hungarian origin of my stories. I believed that no one in my town would have a copy of this ancient moth-eaten book and continued to send my contributions and collect my cheque month after month.

But I went cold all over and shivered in the height of summer one day when I accidentally saw in a local bookshop huge parcels containing the very same book in colourful paperback! That ended my literary career rather abruptly.

Next, I found a job, of all places, in a firm of building contractors. They treated me with great respect because I was the only literate person in their whole set-up. I was hard-working and efficient and therefore pampered with liberal leave of absence and frequent pleasant surprises in my pay packet. On such occasions I acted out my gratitude so demonstratively that it moved the two partners greatly and I further gained their confidence.

But the truth was that the salary they gave was not the only source of my income. The real money came from the cement bags I used to squirrel away from the firm's godown and unload in the black market! The transactions were brisk and the fortunes large, unmanageably large, I would say! To avoid a dangerous inundation of money at home I had to buy a good deal of immovable property of all kinds and gift my wifereal diamond and gold jewellery. I was always elegantly dressed and smoked expensive cigars.

All this was very well as far as it went but the tension and risk that my clandestine business involved began to wear me down. I lived in constant dread of being caught while delivering the stolen cement bags to my clients.

However, it was amazing how God always took my side although my relation with Him had never been closer than that between a family and its family doctor, who never came into the picture as long as everyone enjoyed good health. As if in answer to my desperate wish I ran into a fellow whom I had always envied: he lived as well as I did but surprisingly without seeming to move a muscle in his body. It was he who revealed to me over several glasses of beer the blessings of the government's licensing system in regard to imports of certain essential items required by various manufacturing firms in the country. My good friend taught me how to procure these licenses.

Soon my interest in cornering cement bags vanished. Now I was busy running up to Delhi almost thrice a week to meet the officials of various ministries, their deputies, clerks and even their peons. Soon my sleek leather handbag bulged with all sorts of government licenses and permits obtained, of course, on fictitious grounds. But to those who genuinely needed them in a hurry I was a benefactor: it was easier and quicker to come to me rather than to go through the tortuous bureaucratic channels.

Thus I became a hawker of licenses and found the occupation almost respectable and even legitimate compared to blackmarketing in cement bags.

I needed a name for my business and after a lot of thinking chose one which had about it a ring of dignity and age. In a congested locality I hired a small room just enough for a table and couple of rickety chairs. I dumped bundles of dog-eared dummy files and nailed a signboard on the door announcing the office of the 'Eastern Equipment and Machinery Ltd.' I hung up cheap prints of our national leaders and heroes on the walls and garlanded them with handspun cotton yarn. In this way I succeeded in giving my place of operation an appallingly drab look. But it passed off for years of unrewarded honesty and struggle! I reinforced this impression by moving among my fellow men wearing a harried look all the time and volubly criticizing the government's policy of stifling controls which really were my bread and butter.

Gradually I woke up to the fact that I could move still further afield. The country bristled with shortages: foodstuffs, trucks, fertilizers, tyres, synthetic yarns, printing paper, kerosene, baby-food, sugar, drugs. Nearly every item of daily use seemed to offer me amazing gains. It would be utter stupidity, I thought, if I did not take the opportunity that the government, the producer and the consumer were bent on giving me so generously.

Hardly a couple of months after I saw this munificent vision I was riding all over the town in an obscenely expensive imported car. I also now possessed extensive property scattered in various parts of the country including a cottage tucked away in a tea estate in Ooty. The house I lived in was the talk of the town: its shape was abstract and futuristic as if Martian architects had been specially summoned to build it. One of the most expensive decorators in the country had attended to the interior of the house. The wizard had created sheer fantasy in chromium, plastic and velvet. I specially commissioned an artist to do a life-size portrait of Gandhiji in oils for my drawing-room.

I despatched both my sons to the USA: one to study business management and the other to take a degree in electrical engineering. As for me, well, I had become a very important social figure.

I spent my evening sipping whisky with an air of superior boredom at cocktail parties. Of course, my hosts and hostesses were invariably flattered by my presence. Rattling icecubes in my glass I would rub shoulders with real tycoons of industry who had ulcers caused by real worries and tensions. Occasionally, at such parties, I came across a few representatives of the people, I mean, members of parliament and state legislative assemblies, self-consciously clutching a glass of some innocuous-looking drink. Moving with them more closely I realized that getting acquainted with people in political circles was the logical next stage in the evolution of the kind of career I had carved out for myself. So I assiduously cultivated them. This automatically led to contacts with more important personalities in the political field. After that it was a quick jump to the higher circle consisting of cabinet ministers and their hangers-on. In course of time I became a close friend and confidant of most of them and even earned the privilege of calling them by their first names.

As a matter of routine I used to pick out a minister for a call in the morning, join him at breakfast and have a casual chat before he departed from the house to set the gigantic wheels of administration in motion.

And I made sure, at the breakfast-table meetings, that those wheels moved in my favour: a government contract for a friend for laying electric cables in a particular project area or for a paint manufacturer for painting a bridge across a river. In all this I got my cut from the contractor and so of course did the honourable minister, in a more devious way.

Now I had gone up really high in the social ladder. The respect my fellow men showed me was tinged with a certain fear because I was frequently seen at public functions seated along with the governor, the mayor or a minister. The press began to consider me newsworthy and included my name or photograph when reporting such functions. I was even invited to address the local Rotary Club once and another time the Junior Chamber of Commerce. I remember having thrown open an art exhibition too.

My main occupation was that of a tout acting for the business community on the one hand and on the other for the powers that be. I was amazed by the number of contracts I was instrumental in securing for various interested parties: the monopoly of plying the passenger-bus service, the construction of the government hospital, the municipal auditorium and various other petty jobs like city road repairs, painting the ironrailings in the parks, supplying drill uniforms to the ward boys in the government hospital and so on.

Money did not interest me any more. I was after power now. I measured it against that of the ministers and derived a curious joy in seeing them buckle under pressure and yield to my suggestion, or fall for the temptation I cunningly held out, or succumb, maybe, to a subtle hint at blackmail.

Slowly the realization came to me—the ministers knew that I knew a little too much for their good! It was at this stage that I lost my peace of mind. I began to feel uneasy in their presence and insecure, as if I was in some sort of a weird secret society from which there was no escape. I imagined that we held each other on an invisible leash of constant watchfulness. Fear made me read all sorts of dreadful meanings into the way they looked at me or talked to me. I desperately wanted to run away from the life I was leading. But I knew it would be disastrous to snap ties with them abruptly—as risky as getting off the back of a maneater. Even mere suspicion on their part would surely destroy me. But thankfully no one had the slightest inkling of what was going on in my mind.

To cut the story short, philanthropy, in a roundabout way, helped me finally to withdraw to a pious world of harmless activities, far from the reach of contractors, commissions, and ministers.

I financed a free primary school and named it after my mother. I added a separate ward to the local hospital with beds and all and named it after my father. I created a trust that would award scholarships to deserving students for higher studies, expanded and equipped the medical college laboratory and started a charity home for single mothers. Somehow all this created an agreeable gap between me and all those characters I wanted to avoid.

At this time the general elections in the country was announced and that made my total disappearance from the scene easier. Except for a little house and a few acres of land in my remote ancestral village I quickly sold every bit of my property and liberally gave away the proceeds to a variety of political parties regardless of their shade and colour. The election activities were steadily gathering momentum and working towards a delirious pitch. It was at that point I left the town quietly with my wife.

I have lived happily in my village for several years now. I have a comfortable house; not too big, not too small. I have a car and a few servants. My wife likes the quiet life we lead. My elder son is the chief technical adviser to a huge industrial complex and the younger son is prospering as a management consultant for a string of firms. Of course, I do nothing much these days except spend the time in the open air under the blue sky, looking at my green paddy fields and watching the interlacing of my grapevines as they inch up the poles. Thus I enjoy a great sense of well-being and contentment for which I am grateful to the Almighty, and also to the country for all the opportunities it gave.

BAREFOOT IN THE PALACE

I WAS shown into a small room through a side entrance. But for the guard at the door in his gold-embroidered red uniform gripping a savagely huge sword, it was hard to believe that I was inside one of the biggest palaces in the country.

There was, of course, an oil portrait on the wall of the ruler dressed in a complicated blend of British and Indian regal splendour. Next to it a notice painted on a wooden plank announced, 'All people other than Europeans should remove their footwear including socks here before entering the palace . . . ' Or something to that effect.

I carried out the order and got ready to follow my escort. I had put on my best shirt, tie and suit for the occasion but now I felt silly and naked without my shoes on.

For the next quarter of an hour we kept going through innumerable arches, corridors, pillared halls, up flights of stairs, under giant chandeliers and along murals of battle scenes huge as a hockey field. All the way I waded through acres of fifteen-ply lush carpets, sinking up to my knees.

At the end of it we came to a hall which looked something like a royal Chor-Bazaar: crystal glassware, paintings of English country life, Chinese scrolls, Rajput miniatures, ancient clocks, musical instruments and stuffed birds and tigers. Here I was asked to wait and offered a seat which was the most expensive I had ever sat upon.

So ornate was it with gold-laced velvet bolsters, pearl tassels and silver filigree work, I felt I was sitting on a bejewelled dowager.

At a slightly elevated level on a throne, his cheeks ruddy, whiskers battle-ready, sat the ruler of the land in wax. But he was measured, tinted and dressed up in royal robes to approximate, except for life, to the nearest degree the original of some half a century ago.

The glassy eyes stared eternally out of the window at the green pastures of the sprawling palace estate where at that point of time the royal dairy buffaloes were grazing, merrily twitching their tails. The escort returned to lead me on my further journey. I nearly bade goodbye to His Late Highness when I left the room.

More corridors, pillars, chandeliers and halls and we came to a door big enough to let an elephant pass, howdah, king, and all. Fierce-looking guards stood as if frozen on either side with spears curved like the crescent moon.

The door opened, revealing an enormous hall: officials of the royal court were bowing and at the same time walking backwards towards the exit. Once out, they stood erect and walked away normally.

Then it was my turn to be conducted to the presence of His Highness. I felt silly and naked without my shoes on as I went in.

AS LIFE UNFOLDS . . .

FOR ME the day begins as it does for many others, with the unfolding of the morning paper.

The very thought of having to read, understand, and extract sense out of the spew of events, speeches, policies and plans makes me desperately want to run away to a tiny cottage with a view of blue mountains in some remote jungle, to enjoy a life of undisturbed tranquillity.

But these are bad thoughts to occur early in the morning, especially if one happens to be the bread winner of the family. Eventually, I have got to get up, rush off to the office and plunge myself into more newspapers. So I brush aside this defeatist vision; there is a whole world waiting for me to set right through my cartoons and I cannot shirk my responsibility. But I see there are a few more minutes yet. Let me make the best of them.

I avoid the calamity columns and turn the pages to the classified advertisements. I cannot resist the vicarious joy of reading about the eternal foreigner who is leaving this country and who wants to sell his binoculars, cooking range and icebucket. Odd things, indeed, to be left with, I should imagine, after half a decade's spectacular career in India. I like to speculate on him and his life of comfort here with chauffeurs, servants and golf—the home he is going back to, is I am sure, cold, colourless, and drab.

But my line of thought is interrupted; my eyes catch an advertisement under 'Miscellaneous'. It quietly announces: ' . . . Four-track, three-speed, three magnetic hands, two loudspeakers, latest, brand-new, unpacked unused tape recorder for sale . . .' At once my suspicions are aroused; why did he buy it in the first place if he was going to keep it unpacked and unused? Surely there is something fascinatingly shady about this man's business. In my mind's eye I can see him sporting a pair of dark glasses, he has fancy whiskers and sideburns, and he smokes cigarettes in an ivory holder. Before I can further thicken the plot of this mystery, a huge advertisement on another page captures my attention. It shows a family of four with angelic faces in ecstatic joy and an exploding message at the bottom which says, 'ALL YOUR PROBLEMS ARE OVER!'

I can never cease marvelling at the people in the advertisement. They seem so totally exempt from all the ills and suffering that assail humanity such as floods, earthquakes, poverty, cold, bad breath, backache and baldness. However, the advertisement which attracts me now is about a new brand of biscuit; the whole handsome family is not merely engaged in crunching the delectable stuff but adoring it too!

It warms my heart to see such completely happy people who seem to have discovered a solution for all human woes in an ordinary biscuit. Ironically, there is a news item next to this advertisement about some poor secondary school teachers on a protest fast. I cannot help the thought that these disgruntled gentlemen ought to partake of those miracle biscuits in the next column!

Such idle, frivolous thinking is a luxury one is entitled to before one wakes up fully to face the painful realities of the outside world. I come across one of them the moment I reach the corner of the street in my car. The mammoth traffic jam throbbing with impatience and giving out dark fumes, looks like a stubborn beast with a life of its own.

On such hopeless occasions I settle down to scrutinize my fellow drivers in other cars and their occupants, pedestrians and harassed policemen. The rugged-looking taxi driver on my right has wisely switched off the engine of his battered taxi and has dozed off in his seat. Next to the taxi is the shiny little car of a junior executive, I should think, of a prosperous firm, judged by his natty tie, watch and hairdo. He is looking anxiously at his watch and the impenetrable traffic jam ahead and, every now and then, looks round in despair. I have seen this young man for many years at the same spot at the same time going through the same act.

Then there is the old gentleman with the profile of Julius Caesar in the black sedan. He is another familiar sight at this corner. He is always seen concentrating calmly on the crossword in the morning paper, sitting buried deep in the rear seat. I have watched him thus for years and noted his hair turn from black to steel grey to snow-white.

Similarly, over the years I have seen in a bus queue a lissome lass metamorphose into the hefty matron that she is today, standing there patiently in the same position in the queue.

It is sad that our lives have thus come to be regulated like clockwork, minus all the excitement of fresh sights and new experiences. Even the road accidents which one would expect to produce shock are viewed as a familiar sight.

In other matters too we are reduced to a dull state of perpetual anticipation like looking at a movie which we have seen over and over. For instance, at any public function—whether it is foundation laying or statue unveiling—everyone know what the presiding dignitary is going to say, nor will anyone be surprised if he arrives a couple of hours late. Haven't we all come to expect as a matter of routine, scans, mismanagement, irregularities, misuse of funds and finally a judicial enquiry around any project? Likewise, no normal person in the present-day world will feel scandalized to learn that the vice-chancellor of a university is bullied and stoned by his students or that the chairman of a company is locked up in his toilet by his employees.

In short, life from the moment one wakes up to the moment one retires at night is a succession of stereotyped experiences. This sort of apparently unexciting existence suits my temperament eminently. It leaves me free to discover and enjoy the out-of-the-ordinary in the common day-to-day routine.

I do not have to listen to the man in front of the mike for I already know what he is going to say. I use my time observing his mannerisms, studying the way he fiddles with the third button on his coat, remembering his long nose, short chin, bald pate and other interesting details, all of which I will use profitably in a caricature. Thank heavens, no two faces are alike and I can have endless delight whether I am in a vegetable market or at a wedding reception.

Similarly, politics is a dull, cliché-ridden business and here too I look for the oddities and awkwardness that the people engaged in it are so inclined to reveal. I hear one of them say, 'Our economy has turned the corner; we are now at last, in a position to face our financial crisis . . .' Another asserts, 'I am agreeable to arbitration if I am assured that the dispute will be settled in my favour.' Yet one more shouts indignantly, 'Your strike is illegal and unreasonable! I will not yield to your demands for another four or five days.' And lastly, I hear a thundering voice proclaim, 'We all belong to one nation . . . and we are all Indian first, especially the people of our region who will not rest till a separate state is given to them . . .'

Thus, I look forward to another day to derive a thrill out of a dull morning paper, seek variety in a tedious traffic jam, enchantment out of human faces and fun in a humdrum life.

SILENT DAYS

ON THE CONGESTED narrow street in front of the Theatre Royal a five-piece brass band was pouring out some vague noisy notes. A man in shirt and dhoti with a bagpipe which had genuine Scottish tartan trimmings tucked under his arms was squeezing out, as he paced up and down, a sad Highland marching tune. Oddly, all this noise and the smell of sliced cucumbers and fried peanuts that lingered in the air created for us, in those days of silent movies in our village, the atmosphere of the Wild West, lusty cowboys, gun-smoke, stallions galloping across the rugged terrain of Arizona.

At the entrance to the theatre there was a wooden board pinned on to which were 'stills'. We gazed at them fascinated, trying to conjure up the situation that led up to a man being readied under a tree for hanging or a horse majestically clearing the space between two deadly cliffs with the rider and his lady love. We would be brought back to reality with a jerk by the sound of a bell asking us to get in.

Inside, we spoke in hushed tones and looked over our shoulders discreetly at those in the upper class as if afraid of violating the propriety that the Theatre Royal expected of its patrons.

The screen, of course, was small but its setting was elaborate. It was framed in an enormous drove of winged angels and cherubs cast in plaster, playfully engaged in paying floral tribute to the rectangular white space on which our cowboy would make his appearance.

A bell chimed far away over the din of the crowd around us and all our attention was turned to the balcony which bulged like the laced bosom of a dowager. There a thin, tall, long-haired man in black bow and tuxedo appeared. A hush fell.

He bowed to the audience with extreme grace and took his seat at a piano. Immediately, the doors and windows were shut, black curtains were drawn and lights switched off. Then Beethoven's *Pastorale* filled the hall, drowning the cry of vendors selling paan, beedis and cigarettes.

At last the cowboy came on the screen, galloping across a landscape of jagged rocks and cacti. He rode superbly in tune with the music emanating from the balcony above. As the neatly defined conflict unfolded from adventure to adventure we sat engrossed in the acts of violence, treachery, heroism and romance. The vision on the screen and the sounds produced by our maestro matched so well that for us *The Bad Men of Brimstone* was virtually a talkie much ahead of its time!

We held our breath as the bad guy suddenly made his appearance from behind a rock and with a mean smile took aim with his gun as the unsuspecting hero cantered down a narrow gap in the canyon. Just at this point an announcement was flashed on the screen accompanied by a hysterical crescendo of music: *DO NOT MISS PART TWO ON FRIDAY NEXT*! The lights came on, exposing us suddenly to a painful anticlimax.

Badly let down, we ambled out of the Theatre Royal to the strains of *'God Save The King'*.

THE BESPECTACLED GOAT

WHETHER A FACE is beautiful, plain, comical or villainous it is a fascinating object to watch. Most people take a face for granted and treat it like the address on an envelope. They go about with only a vague impression of their friends, relatives and neighbours. The physical features of a face are not needed for memory. That is why one often wonders whether a person one had met the previous day had a moustache or not, whether he wore glasses at all, whether he parted his hair on the left or the right. Yet if one happens to meet him again the recognition is almost immediate. When we remember a face it is the personality of the individual we recall to memory and not its details.

There was a time when the cartoonist had an easy time drawing popular world figures. Churchill generously lent his famous cigar to the caricaturist with which he could be symbolized and, perhaps, even be dispensed with altogether, drawing only the cigar.

Stalin had his formidable whiskers. Hitler, his tooth-brush moustache. Nearer home Rajaji's dark glasses, Gandhiji's . . . well, he wholly offered himself to the caricaturist, and Jinnah's monocle, cigarette-holder, and extraordinary physical thinness were all pegs for the caricaturist to hang his talent on.

But the times have changed and now the caricaturist bemoans the departure of these colourful characters from the world stage. No aggressive characteristics are sported any more. On this basis Mrs Gandhi, Reagan, Mrs Thatcher or Vajpayee have nothing very interesting about them that could be reduced to a simple recognizable symbol. But a true cartoonist does not merely depend on eyebrows or a beard or the shape of the chin. He seeks a factor beyond the physical side and that is where the oddity lies and that is what goes into his caricature of a face. A normal person with an air of regal dignity about him could be made to look like Mickey Mouse without destroying his recognizable appearance. The art of caricature has revealed that the line that divides the silly and the solemn is very thin indeed.

Long years in this business has taught me that there does exist a strange likeness, however remote and far-fetched, between people and animals, birds and, with a further stretch of imagination, even inanimate objects. I do not find it difficult at all, for instance, to correlate the resemblance of a particular person to an old ramshackle truck or T-Model Ford, or the appearance of a cabinet minister to a particular bottle in a drug store. I know a person whose wife unfailingly reminded me of the Taj Mahal by moonlight!—of course, suggested by her make-up, size, jewellery, etc. It is these ridiculous associations of ideas that help the caricaturist. I discovered this secret when I was a boy.

Our home in Mysore used to get a lot of magazines. They lay scattered on a table in the hall and I used to spend hours going through them as they contained a lot of pictures of people, places, trees, mountains and animals. Our neighbours used to constantly drop in to collect a magazine or two for weekend reading. Sometimes they would return them dog-eared and begrimed and sometimes, mercifully, not return them at all. However, in course of time the periodicals disappeared, making room, like the change of seasons, for new arrivals.

I was constantly busy drawing pictures wherever I could in those days; walls, doors, sheets of paper in my father's desk and even the margins and endpapers of deluxe edition of classics were all covered with drawings of trees, the rising sun, cottages, crows, funny portraits of men, women and children, etc.

I used to derive particular delight in distorting the photographs in the magazines, adding curly moustaches to the pretty face of a winner of a beauty contest, or *namams* to a formidable-looking Nazi, or giving hats to those who did not have them or goggles or turbans; and so on I went merrily. My elders allowed me this liberty only with the magazines that had outlived their use on the table. I think I found *Life* magazine particularly good for my purpose.

One day I was busy adding a pair of horn-rimmed glasses to a picture of a very attractive goat found in the Ural mountains. Sitting next to me was a friend of our family. This gentleman never took the magazines home but read them all in the cool comfort of our drawing room, taking his own time. After satisfying myself with my efforts on the goat, I moved on to other magazines. For hours we sat together silently absorbed in our respective activities.

Suddenly, he jumped up and shouted at me, in what seemed uncontrollable rage which shook the house and brought the elders hurrying to us. He was at that moment holding the *Life* magazine at the page showing the bespectacled goat. 'I will never again step into this house after this insult!' he roared, hurling the magazine to the floor, and walked out. We stood petrified and bewildered, not having a clue as to what it was all about! My elder brother recovered from the shock a bit and picked up the magazine to find out what triggered the family friend's outrage. He examined the goat for some time, turned to me with a smile and said, 'You should not do this sort of thing. Poor man!'

Looking at the humanized goat, I myself was astonished to discover the remarkable resemblance to our erstwhile friend of the family! Accidentally, I had stumbled at that moment on the key to the art of caricature.

Even now I look at a face beyond the physical shape, light and shade, or colour of the skin, for that undefinable, elusive, surprise element which a face actually hides and which is so essential for caricature.

THE DISTORTED MIRROR

PEOPLE ARE CURIOUS about my profession and try to clear their doubts by putting all sorts of questions. Recently a lady asked me, 'Do you do the drawings for your cartoons yourself?' I answered, 'Yes, I do.' Then she questioned, 'And the captions to the cartoons, do you write them too?' 'Of course,' I said. And, finally, she asked, 'The ideas for the cartoons, don't say you think them up too?' Of course, this kind of dialogue is an extreme example. But of all the questions the one that is frequently put to me is how I get my ideas. It is impossible to give a serious answer to this and so I usually evade it by some supposedly funny rejoinder. The other questions are: How big are the original cartoons? How long do I take to do them? How many people work under me? What do the ministers think of my making fun of them? Do they have a sense of humour? Have I ever been arrested and if not why not?—and so on. For all such questions I give replies ranging from the flippant to the scholarly, depending on the questioners, their interest and mood.

There is one that is rather rarely asked but which makes me go into deep introspection. This is: 'When you look around, does everything appear funny to you?'

A cartoonist does not lead a charmed life of perpetual fun out of the reach of the cares and worries that bedevil his fellow men. The fluctuating prices of onions affect me in the same way as they delight or outrage a primary schoolteacher. Likewise, taxes depress my spirit. Bores at the mike, and traffic jams drive me crazy. Surely a doctor does not always look at life in terms of coughs, colds, allergies and bronchial inflammations. A star of the silver screen, I am sure, has enough sense to know that beyond the range of the camera life does not continue to be full of idyllic scenes, sex, songs and ketchup-blood. Why, then, should a cartoonist see living caricatures and hear rib-tickling dialogue all around him? So I comfort myself with the self-assurance that my view of life is normally as banal as that of the next man in the queue for sugar or kerosene.

But I do sometimes wonder at the back of my mind whether my profession has not had a subtle influence on my outlook. After officially closing down for the day, I do keep on searching for ideas and oddities subconsciously through all my waking hours.

That is why I like to watch faces and entertain myself standing at a streetcorner as if it were a gallery of portraits in three dimensions. From the eighteen-year-old filly dancing on the other side of the road to the grubby-looking beggar at my heels whose face is hewn out by the weather and anxiety, and scores of others passing by, I am fascinated to see them all.

This occupational pastime is not confined just to observing the oddities in the physical features of a person. The habit wanders into wider fields and there is a great deal of fun to be derived from studying human character which is beyond the reach of the caricaturist's pencil and is captured only in terms of verbal descriptions. Most people seem either dull, cantankerous, pompous, egoistical or plain stupid to most other people. But a modicum of tolerance and objectivity will reveal in all of them the lovable eccentric.

For instance, a friend of mine became the object of intense hostility over nearly two square miles of our locality because our entire neighbourhood suddenly discovered that he was vainglorious, vulgar, egoistic and despicable. All that he did was celebrate his fiftieth birthday in rather a grand style and in a manner as if no one in the world had ever achieved his type of greatness. He had film music blaring out from loudspeakers turned towards the road right from the early hours of the historic day. He had festooned the trees and potted plants with blinking coloured lights. He served ice-cream and eatables in keepsake cups and plates embossed with his name and age! My reaction to this person was different from those of my friends. His self-glorification did not revolt me. Rather, it amused me and he seemed to me not a wicked fellow but a funny one. He was a character I liked to watch.

Another equally interesting character whose company I thoroughly enjoy is a professor of a university, a peerless authority in his field but generally considered by others a crashing bore! He has this urge to project himself into every conversation, whatever the subject under discussion. He would say, 'Yes, yes, I remember once I was in Geneva,' for a casual remark that the weather is getting to be pretty warm. 'It was a particularly nasty winter. I had been invited to a conference, you see. I was one of the four top people to address the conference. It was there that I made the famous statement that . . .

I always enjoy his company and sit waiting with eager expectation to see with what ingenuity he would work into each subject that came up in the course of the conversation. Once he asked me how I got the ideas for my cartoons and how I set about my work. He seemed so earnest and interested that I decided to take some pains to explain. But even before I had cleared my throat to begin, he started to describe his own daily routine: his morning walks, the evening cigars, the reading posture, the method of preparing for his classroom lectures and so on. At the end he

said he was glad to learn so much about my work!
This man is looked upon by others as a dreadful blight
on social conversation. But I like his company. I can
spend hours with him without getting bored, leading
him on from the subject of disarmament to dandruff,
then on to road repairs and sea voyages and await
with suppressed delight his grand entry into each
subject.

There is another character I frequently run into.
This one is tall and thin and reminds me curiously of
a razor. His eyes are perenially red as if he has just
come out of a fight. He is usually found at all cultural
events sitting in the first row, whether it is music,
dance, a puppet show or a play. One would think he
was there to enjoy the evening. But no, such pleasures
are for the philistines! He is a purist and believes in
flagellation! He will sit there listening to the music
and wince and squirm in his seat as if he were
witnessing a bloody murder while his neighbours enjoy
the performance with open-mouthed admiration. At
the end of the programme he will come out, his eyes
redder, still seething with rage, and announce that he
felt like breaking the musical instrument over the head
of the artist or choking the vocalist for ruining the
musical composition, or for pronouncing the words
wrong, or for being too slow or too fast. For him our
ancient art of dancing is dead and what we have today
in its place is a mere circus and it should be banned

and the impostors prosecuted! According to this suffering aesthete all actors are hams, all paintings are a huge hoax played on the public and all forms of art are dead and what thrives today are only devices to torture his soul.

I can recall many more such interesting types, proving thereby perhaps, in conclusion, that my normal vision is tinted by my profession after all! The world is, no doubt, full of serious-minded, decent, sane people who go to work, earn a living and take care of their families. But it would be a pretty drab world indeed if they really are what they seem and not a bit like what a cartoonist makes them out to be.